Avenged

Also by Jay Crownover

Go to https://www.jaycrownover.com/ for more information

Avenged
By Jay Crownover

A MacKenzie Family Novella

Introduction by Liliana Hart

EVIL EYE
CONCEPTS

Avenged
A MacKenzie Family Novella
Copyright 2017 Jay Crownover
ISBN: 978-1-942299-78-3

Introduction copyright 2017 Liliana Hart

Published by Evil Eye Concepts, Incorporated

Author's Note

First off, I have to tell you how excited I was when Liliana contacted me to take on this project. Authors are very protective of their worlds and their characters, as they should be. Those words are our everything; we guard them with every fiber of our beings. They're an extension of us, a peek into our minds and hearts…so being allowed to play with Liliana's baby was a big deal and an honor I didn't take lightly. I also couldn't say YES fast enough when she asked. I have a real fondness for romantic suspense, for love stories with a bite, so having her open the door for me to readers that embrace nothing less is an opportunity I couldn't wait to sink my teeth into. I really adore Liliana (she was one of the very first authors that approached me and struck up a conversation well before I had the bestseller title attached to my name), and I really love this series and every single one of her badass boys, so I hope that I did her words and her world justice.

All of that being said, if you are new to my work there are characters in this story that appear in two of my existing series (don't worry, there are several MacKenzies that pop in throughout). The main love story can definitely be read as a standalone, but the overall plotline ties into the end of my book HONOR and is kind of a bridge to the next book in the series, DIGNITY (the Breaking Point series). Many of the Point characters are at play here. There are also several appearances from characters that are in my book BUILT (The Saints of Denver series). This is a crossover novella that spans 3 separate worlds, so I know my longtime readers will get a kick out of it, but I am also aware that it is a lot of info for new readers to take in. My hope is that I told a story that was engaging and interesting enough that if you don't know who the other characters are who show up throughout, that you'll want to know more about them by the end. And if not, I'm 100% certain Benny and Echo have enough chemistry and conflict to keep you entertained during their time in Surrender.

For my die-hard readers, I hope you have as much fun with this mashup as I did while I was writing it. There is something about tying loose ends into an unlikely and messy bow that really makes me happy.

Thanks for reading…

Love & Ink

Jay

Author Acknowledgments

First I want to thank Liliana Hart for inviting me to this project. It was really fun and such a wonderful opportunity.

I want to shout out to Liz Berry and Jillian Stein for being two of the smartest, savviest women I know…they also happen to be two of the funniest, wackiest humans on the planet; don't let their million dollar accessories fool you.

I need to thank Mel for always stepping up and wrangling me when I need it. When I'm working on a thousand projects at once, that means she's working on a thousand projects at once…on top of having a full and active life.

I want to thank Mike for keeping my day to day together when it feels like it is splitting apart at the seams. Thank you for keeping me grounded in reality, dude…also, thanks for taking one for the team and going to the occasional chick-flick with me.

I always owe my parents a bucket of gratitude. They are unwavering in their support of me, regardless of what I'm writing. My mom may have even been the one to encourage me to go my own way when I was starting to feel trapped and beaten down by my circumstances.

My tribe…I love them. I admire them. I aspire to be like them. I wouldn't be where I am today without them. When you find the people that get you, the ones that keep it real and don't ever let you fall, but pick you up when you do, hold onto them and never take them for granted.

For you readers, thank you for following me into uncharted territory! It's an adventure you won't regret taking…I promise.

To all the bloggers and book pimps…I appreciate all you do. Thank you for holding the book world together and for creating a safe space for romance lovers of all kinds.

Want to touch base with me? These are all the places you can find me.

You should sign up for my newsletter right now so you don't miss a thing! It's full of everything I'm currently working on and everything I have planned for the immediate future.

http://www.jaycrownover.com/subscribe

You can also appease your inner stalker in all of these places:

https://www.facebook.com/groups/crownoverscrowd… My fan group on Facebook. I'm very active in there and often the best place to find all the happenings and participate in giveaways!

www.jaycrownover.com...there is a link on the site to reach me through email.

https://www.facebook.com/jay.crownover

https://www.facebook.com/AuthorJayCrownover

Follow me @jaycrownover on Twitter

Follow me @jay.crownover on Instagram

https://www.goodreads.com/Crownover

http://www.donaghyliterary.com/jay-crownover.html

http://www.avonromance.com/author/jay-crownover

An Introduction to the Mackenzie Family World

Dear Readers,

I'm thrilled to announce the MacKenzie Family World is returning! I asked five of my favorite authors to create their own characters and put them into the world you all know and love. These amazing authors revisited Surrender, Montana, and through their imagination you'll get to meet new characters, while reuniting with some of your favorites.

These stories are hot, hot, hot and packed with action and adventure—exactly what you'd expect from a MacKenzie story. It was pure pleasure for me to read each and every one of them and see my world through someone else's eyes. They definitely did the series justice, and I hope you discover five new authors to put on your auto-buy list.

Make sure you check out Spies and Stilettos, a brand new, full-length MacKenzie novel written by me. This will be the final installment of the MacKenzie series, featuring Brady Scott and Elena Nayal. After eighteen books of my own and ten books written by other bestselling authors in the MacKenzie World, it's going to be difficult to say goodbye to a family I know as well as my own. Thank you for falling in love with the MacKenzies.

So grab a glass of wine, pour a bubble bath, and prepare to Surrender.

Love Always,
Liliana Hart

* * * *

Available now!
Trouble Maker by Liliana Hart
Rush by Robin Covington

Bullet Proof by Avery Flynn
Delta: Rescue by Cristin Harber
Deep Trouble by Kimberly Kincaid
Desire & Ice by Christopher Rice

Spies & Stilettos by Liliana Hart
Never Surrender by Kaylea Cross
Avenged by Jay Crownover
Hot Witness by Lynn Raye Harris
Wicked Hot by Gennita Low
Hollow Point by Lili St. Germain

Chapter 1

Echo

I was cold.

Freezing.

Frigid all the way down to my bones. Bones that ached and throbbed under my icy skin from the impact of my sporty little SUV sliding off the winding mountain road and into a nearby ravine. I wasn't sure how many times the vehicle had flipped over, but I could clearly recall my panic and fear as I frantically turned the steering wheel every direction to try and break the skid and to stop the nightmare that was quickly unfolding in front of my eyes. I was born and raised in Denver, Colorado, so winter driving was nothing new to me. I had four-wheel drive and was overly confident that winters in Montana couldn't be any worse than winters in the Mile High.

I was wrong. Really fucking wrong.

I'd never seen so much snow fall in the span of an hour. Everything was white: the road, the shoulder, the sky, my entire windshield. It was a whiteout in a matter of minutes and when the wind picked up, it was like I was trying to drive through a snow globe someone wouldn't stop shaking. Montana was also far less populated than Colorado. Even up in the mountains where I was from, you would stumble across a little ski town or spread of ranches every fifty miles or so. Montana wasn't like that. It was...vast. There were stretches and stretches of road that seemed to lead nowhere and along the way there was nothing but the wildlife and intimidating snowdrifts that warned of what was coming—if only I had paid attention.

The wheels of my SUV hit black ice coming around a particularly nasty switchback. The car started to slide toward the edge of the mountain and I knew there was nothing I could do to regain control, but that didn't stop me from trying. I did everything I wasn't supposed to do in that situation: slammed the brakes, jerked the wheel, and closed my eyes as I braced for the inevitable impact. Unfortunately, my SUV had big, knobby snow tires on it, so when I hit the battered guardrail that was supposed to save my life, I bounced off of it and toppled over it like a Ping-Pong ball. The car was upside down and sliding down the embankment with one jarring impact after another. The windshield shattered, covering me in glass, and the metal of the roof groaned and shrieked as the force of it hitting the ground sent it crumpling inwards toward my head. The airbag deployed with enough force that I couldn't breathe when it hit me right in the nose. My chest jerked against my seatbelt so hard that I screamed when the nylon cut into my shoulder and the side of my neck. I could smell blood and gasoline, but over it all I could smell the acrid scent of my fear.

It was seconds—maybe a minute at the most—but it felt like forever for the car to stop flipping. It ended up on its roof, the still-spinning wheels pointed at the night sky as the engine whined and my breath puffed out in white clouds into the chilly Montana air. I could vaguely make out the trunk of a massive tree that had stopped the crash from taking me all the way down to the bottom of the ravine. Everything was on an angle and my long, dark hair was hanging down in my face as blood rushed to my head, making it difficult to see, or to think straight. I turned my head toward the passenger seat, where my purse and overnight bag had been throughout the drive and wasn't surprised when the seat came up empty. The car had rolled and rolled. If I hadn't been wearing my seatbelt, I would have been thrown out the same way my things had been.

Groaning as I moved my hand to release the clasp of the seatbelt, I saw stars and searing pain shot through my shoulder and down to my fingertips. Everything was slippery with my blood as I worked to get myself free. I knew I couldn't stay dangling upside down in a car that could work its way free at any moment and take me with it to the bottom of the mountain.

It was a painstaking task, one that had fire and acid burning along all my nerve endings, but I got the seatbelt off and managed to catch myself before I smashed into the jagged and sharp pieces of the destroyed roof that were sticking up like razor blades. Getting out through the annihilated windshield didn't go as well. I was having a hard time seeing straight and keeping my balance. My thoughts got heavy and my vision went foggy. I caught my palms on the rough edge where there was still glass and felt my skin break. I also felt the sharp pieces poke through the material of my jeans and dig into my knees, but none of that stopped me. I was nothing if not determined.

In my life, I'd had to be.

Every few months it seemed like I was recovering from one disaster or catastrophe after another. I'd never had anything easy and my life was the opposite of smooth sailing. If you asked my parents, I deserved it for all the trouble I'd caused when I was younger. I didn't agree. Sure, I'd always been a handful and marched to the beat of my own drum, after fucking the drummer, but when that tune turned sour and led me down a dark path, I'd done everything in my power to clean up my act. I had earned a break, I deserved some peace of mind…but it looked like the universe didn't agree.

This was the worst day of my life.

I'd buried my baby sister and almost died running away from grief and guilt.

Once I was free of the car, I flopped on my back on the fluffy blanket of white that covered the surrounding ground. The chill of the snow immediately sank through my clothes and, while it worked to numb the parts of me that were blazing hot with pain, it also dropped the temperature along the rest of my body in no time. I began shivering so hard that I thought my teeth were going to chatter out of my mouth.

I was wearing jeans, a thermal, and a flannel shirt over that. I had on sturdy leather boots that were decorated with cute silver studs. Somewhere in my SUV, if it hadn't been thrown out, was a puffy coat with a fur-trimmed hood that was perfect for this kind of weather. I didn't think I could pull myself up to go find it. Everything hurt and I was cold…colder than I had ever been in my life and that included the way my heart had turned to ice when I found out that within months of losing my best friend to bad decisions, I'd lost my baby sister as well. So much loss. All of it unnecessary. I thought I was never going to be warm again, but I never considered it was possible to get colder.

Blood was pooling around my head, staining the pristine snow scarlet. I could feel the thick liquid rolling over my temple and into my hair and no matter how fast I blinked, I couldn't keep my eyes clear. I wasn't sure where the blood was coming from, but there sure as fuck was a lot of it.

I lay there long enough that I started to collect snow. The flakes got caught in my eyelashes and melted with each blink. I could see the fluffy piles building up on my chest and on the tips of my boots. I knew I had to move, but the idea made everything hurt and it was so much easier to simply lie there and pretend nothing was happening.

It would be so easy to drift away. That was what my best friend had done, even though she had a little boy she was leaving behind. It was what my sister had done, even though she knew I wouldn't be able to handle it and that our parents would inevitably blame me for her taking her own life. It seemed so much easier to let go when hanging on required so much more effort.

An owl hooted from somewhere overhead and somewhere in the darkness there was a lonely howl that had to belong to a wolf that broke through the eerie silence. It was a reminder that you were either predator or prey and I wasn't ever going to be the type of woman that let herself be hunted down. I was a fighter through and through—which meant I had to put the effort into hanging on and getting up. I refused to let go of anything.

When my best friend died because she chose to be in the wrong place at the wrong time with absolutely the wrong man, I did everything I could to find her son the best home possible. I wanted to keep him—I loved him like he was my own—but with my past and the glaring mistakes in it, there was no way the state was going to let me do that. They put him in foster care, ready to call it a day, but I was determined that Hyde would have better. I tracked down his father, a giant, bearded badass my bestie had indulged in an illicit one-night stand with, and sprang the news on him that he was a daddy. Of course, I checked the guy out before telling him he had a son. I was pleased to learn that, despite a few hiccups in the past, he was a standup guy, more than willing to give his son a good home.

I also refused to let go of the fact that my baby sister was no longer with me. Xanthe had always been special, a sweet soul who was too trusting and too soft. She was precious and delicate, always a little too fragile and breakable for the reality of the world around her. My entire family did their best to protect her, to shelter her, but Xanthe was like any other twenty-something and she wanted to live. She wanted to experience love and relationships. She wanted to mess up and try again. She wanted to be normal…but the fact of the matter was, she wasn't wired the way the rest of us were. I did my best to protect her while helping her live as normal a life as possible, but that was a full-time job and there were times I couldn't be there. My parents always accused me of encouraging her, of enabling her whims. They swore I was going to be the reason she ended up hurt. I told them she needed professional help, that there was something chemically wrong in her brain. They insisted she was nothing more than a special snowflake that needed to be coddled and loved.

There wasn't any time left for either of those theories because Xanthe was gone, her life stolen away too soon at her own hand. She fell in love, fixated on a man, couldn't let it go, and when he left, she decided she couldn't live without him…even though he'd never encouraged her in any way. She was shattered, fundamentally broken, and forever lost to me.

Now I was bleeding out on the side of a mountain in Surrender, Montana. I'd taken off minutes after the funeral so I could find Xanthe's mystery man and tell him what happened when men weren't careful with delicate hearts. He probably didn't care and it wouldn't change a thing, but for my own peace of mind, I had to say something…had to take a stand for my sister. Her death needed to be avenged and the only way I could do that was to confront the MacKenzie that broke her heart. I didn't have his first name…just his last…but in a town the size of Surrender, I figured it couldn't be that hard to track him down. I'd say what I had to say, make my point, get my own kind of vengeance, and go back to Denver ready to face my parents' wrath. After all, I was the one who'd encouraged Xanthe to get out and get a job so she wouldn't be so melancholy and depressed, so dependent on everyone else for what she needed.

I flipped over to my hands and knees, swearing into the darkness as my left shoulder gave out and left me face-planted in the snow. It hurt worse than anything I'd ever felt before and there was no way I was going to be able to use it. The burn made my eyes cross and had me sucking frigid air through my teeth. I lifted myself up onto my knees and squinted into the shadowy forest as I heard a twig snap and the sound of heavy footfalls. My breaths were suddenly annoyingly loud as they wheezed in and out of me.

I had no idea what was going to come out of the surrounding trees, but my instincts told me it wasn't going to be something friendly and eager to help.

I was right.

Around a tree twice as big as the one that was holding up my SUV stepped a man. A big man. A burly man. A dark man. An angry man.

He had a shotgun grasped firmly in his hands and a scowl on his face that was easy to read, despite the darkness and the distance that separated us.

The lower half of his face was covered by a dark beard, but his equally dark hair was cut in a style that didn't match his mountain man look. The sides were cut super short with a severe part shaved into a harshly defined and trendy part. The top was longer and slicked up and back in a style that looked like it should be in a watch ad of a high-end fashion magazine. There was also an obnoxiously large gold ring on his middle finger. I could see the glint of diamonds off it as he moved several steps closer to me. The ring was seriously at odds with his heavy canvas jacket and worn jeans. His boots looked expensive but had heavy tread and were the right kind of footwear for trekking up a mountainside in the middle of the night. I wasn't sure why, but they seemed out of place. He seemed out of place.

"Are you okay?" His voice was deep and sounded extra loud in the silence surrounding us.

I lowered my head and couldn't keep back a strangled laugh. "Do I look okay?" He was probably my only option for rescue and I wanted to bite my tongue after the waspish remark. Something about him and his mix-and-match appearance had the hairs on the back of my neck rising.

"How not okay are you?" He sounded faintly amused and if I'd had working use of my arm, I would have flipped him off.

"Dislocated shoulder, possible concussion, various nicks and cuts…I'm pretty sure the top of my head is sliced open from when the roof caved in because I'm still bleeding. I don't think it's anything fatal but I'm an insurance adjuster, not a doctor."

His gaze shifted to the mangled SUV and he let out a low whistle. "I heard the impact from down at my cabin. I figured you would have rolled all the way to the bottom of the mountain. I was planning on finding a body."

I lifted an eyebrow and winced as it made my whole head throb. "Sorry to disappoint you."

He smirked and lifted the rifle he was carrying to his shoulder so he could stroke a hand through his beard. "Can you walk? I'll call the accident in to the sheriff but the roads are bad so I doubt anyone will be able to get up here until sometime tomorrow or the next day. They're shutting the highway down, no way in, no way out for the next few days. You must have been on the road right when they made the call."

I groaned and put a shaking hand to my head as the rough noise made everything throb. "Lucky me."

He took a few steps closer and I squinted up in the darkness so I could really see him. He was alarmingly attractive in a surprisingly polished way. The dark hair led me to believe he would have dark eyes as well, but they weren't. They were a clear and stunning shade of gray. I also had dark hair and light-colored eyes, so I knew how striking the combination could be. People, mostly men trying to get in my pants, complimented my coloring all the time.

He took my breath away. In my pain-addled haze, I also noticed he had a scar that bisected one of his eyebrows, another one off center on his bottom lip, and one that made me gasp because it started below his ear, ran all the way down the side of his neck and across until it disappeared into the collar of his coat. It was raised, still pinkish in color, and brutal looking. It also looked very, very recent. It looked like someone had tried to slit the man's throat and that meant he was more than likely not a man I wanted to be alone in the middle of the woods with, especially if the roads were closing and there was no way for help to get to me. Being isolated with a man that someone hated enough that they tried to kill him was not a wonderful option. Too bad I didn't have many others to choose from at the moment.

"So, can you?" Now he sounded impatient and his thick eyebrows pulled into a frown over those amazing eyes.

"Can I what?"

"Walk? We need to get you out of here and someplace warm. My cabin is a few hundred yards south, so I'll take you there until I can get someone from Surrender up the mountain to collect you."

My trepidation must have shown on my face because his scowl deepened as he growled, "What are your other options, Snow White? You gonna stay out here and freeze to death?"

I lifted a hand to my forehead, where blood continued to trickle over my brow. "I might bleed to death before that."

With a resigned sigh, I did my best to climb to my feet. He didn't offer to help, which annoyed me, even though I wouldn't have taken him up on it. Once I had my feet under me, I lifted my chin so I could look at him with pride and defiance…only as soon as I was upright, everything began to swim and blur together in a nauseating swirl. I gasped, putting my hand out to catch myself as I pitched forward, everything fading to black and slipping away.

The last things I remember were rough hands wrapping around my upper arms and the bite of that big-ass ring as the cold of the metal seeped through the wet fabric of my shirt and into my skin.

He didn't offer to help me up…but he refused to let me fall.

Chapter 2

Ben

I called her Snow White and I wasn't far off the mark.

Hair, almost as dark as my own, trapped innocent snowflakes as her head dangled over my arm where I held her unresponsive body clasped to my chest. Her eyelashes were an obsidian fan that cast a shadow on her milky cheeks. I would bet good money that her lips were normally a ruby red, but at the moment they were tinged blue and tinted red with streaks of blood. Her eyes, when they narrowed and challenged me, were the clearest, deepest blue I had ever seen. I thought nothing on Earth could rival the massive, untouched Montana sky in blueness, but this injured woman's gaze won the prize hands down. Even though she was currently covered in blood and badly shaken from the accident, I could tell she was attractive in a way that might prove to be distracting. When she fell into my arms, literally, I got a handful of soft curves and toned flesh that let me know everything she was working with under her layers of clothing was just as nice as what I could see in the dense darkness surrounding us.

She was a looker, one that had no business being out in the middle of nowhere with a guy like me. One would think she was lucky to have survived such a horrific crash. They wouldn't be saying that if they knew I was the only person available to ride to her rescue.

She might be Snow White, but there was no way in hell I was anything close to Prince Charming, or any fairytale prince, for that matter. Hell, I wasn't even the Huntsman that showed mercy and refused to end an innocent life. I was more along the lines of the Big Bad Wolf. I lay in wait for my prey, ready to pounce, all while wearing a civilized front that very few could see through. I had sharp teeth and even sharper claws and I'd been using both for as long as I could remember.

The old me would eat this girl up without a second thought. I would have left her to her fate in the snow. I was impressed as hell with the way she popped up to her feet, with all types of adorable indignation and sexy pride radiating off of her, even though she was obviously hurting and about to fall over.

I was the old me as recently as this morning.

I was the old me until I looked in the mirror after my shower and finally took the time to examine the still-healing slice across my throat. In a rare moment of clarity, I realized how close I had come to meeting my maker. The wound had been there, healing for months, but today was the day I really saw it and realized I no longer wanted to be the kind of man that deserved to have his throat slit open every time he was distracted and not on the defense. There was no way I would have a halo waiting for me on the other side; I had known that for a long time. It was always bound to be horns and a tail for me because I'd been actively courting my own corner in hell for as long as I could remember. I was the guy that had waterfront property on the lake of fire but I no longer wanted to watch the world burn. Those flames got too close and they were leaving scars on more places than my neck.

I wasn't a guy that deserved a second chance.

I wasn't a guy that deserved redemption.

I wasn't a guy that deserved forgiveness.

I wasn't a guy that deserved compassion or pity.

I wasn't a guy that should have been rewarded with a shot to redo and retry everything I had done wrong…but I was a guy that was given that shot. And for whatever reason this morning, while I was looking in the mirror, I told myself it was time to stop squandering it.

I could be the guy that deserved forgiveness. I just had to work at it…harder than anyone else ever had. That was why I caught the pretty little brunette before she hit the ground. It was also why I bundled her up in my coat and tucked her matted and bloody hair into my wool beanie that was in my pocket before trekking the forty-five minutes over uneven and rough terrain back to the secluded cabin I had been calling home for the last four months.

It was like the universe, or maybe the man down below, had heard my morning vow and put the perfect test in my path. Was I really ready to be a standup guy, a decent human being, a man who actually gave a shit about someone or something other than myself? I couldn't answer that question just yet, but the unconscious woman in my arms sure had good timing. If she'd come crashing down the mountain yesterday, I wouldn't have lifted a finger to help. Yesterday, I was still the old me and that guy was a real fucking bastard. That guy absolutely deserved to have his happy ass dropped a million miles from nowhere, cut off from everything he had ever known. He undeniably deserved being stripped of everything he had fought and killed for. That guy deserved to have no power and no prestige.

That guy also deserved to have his throat slashed and the shit beat out of him while he rotted in prison.

The new me, hopefully, wasn't going to have to watch his back every second of every day. The new me was going to keep his nose clean, make good choices, and fake being an average Joe and a good Samaritan. The new me wasn't going to put himself in situations where both the good guys and the bad guys wanted him dead. The new me sounded like the kind of guy I used to shake down and shake up for my old boss. I wanted to kick my own ass and I hadn't even been the new me for a full twenty-four hours yet.

The babe in my arms let out a little moan and shifted. I had to tighten my hold on her and fight for my balance on the slick and slippery ground under my boots. I was a city boy through and through. When the US Marshals dumped me in this burg that I couldn't even find on a map, it was the first time I'd seen anything as green as the forest of trees around my cabin. The trees where I was from had broken limbs and rotten roots. They were brown and twisted, gray and grungy, just like everything else in the Point. It was the first time I could see stars because here they weren't obscured by smog and pollution. And it was definitely the first time I had ever experienced snow. The Marshals wanted me somewhere remote, somewhere that I would see anyone coming from miles and miles away. They said they wanted me somewhere secure because I was such a valuable asset and everyone and their brother back home thought I was six feet under. They didn't want me pulling an Elvis and coming back from the dead over and over again. I was smart enough to know they wanted me somewhere that I couldn't cause any trouble. Presumed dead or not, I had a lot of connections that I could use to create chaos, so this was a prison, albeit one with a much prettier view than the one they'd sprung me from.

I couldn't be more of a fish out of water if I tried. I was used to tailored suits and Italian leather shoes, not denim, flannel, and boots with heavy tread. I liked expensive cologne and fancy food. Back home, I drove a sports car that hugged the road and cost a small fortune. Here I had a four-by-four with snow tires and a winch on the front of it. I'd also never had a beard in my life. I wasn't even sure I could grow one, but decided I should try. Within the first few weeks of getting dumped on the side of the mountain I had a face full of fuzz that made me look like an entirely different man. The locals knew I didn't belong, but strangers like this girl and the tourists I encountered never gave me a second look. I was just another big, bearded mountain man living life rough and wild. I was forgettable…something I had never been. Something I had sold my soul to the highest bidder to assure I never would be.

The little tart in my arms twitched and those heart-stealing baby blues flickered open as she let out another moan of pain. She needed a doctor and it pissed me off that I couldn't get her to one with the roads being impassable. I could patch her up street style but that gash on the top of her head and the dislocated shoulder were going to require more care than I could give.

"You hanging in there, Snow White?" I was huffing and puffing, partly because the cold was bitter and sharp. It hurt to breathe. I was also not used to hiking through the snow with a load. Every few steps I had to fight to keep my balance so that I didn't drop the woman on her delightfully rounded backside. Back in the city, I was the guy that gave the orders to the younger guys who did the dirty work. I clearly needed to hit a gym and start running a few miles if I was going to get back to my previous fighting form. New me needed to get his ass back in shape.

"Echo."

The word was mumbled and slurred, so I wasn't sure what she was saying. I frowned down at her and tightened my hold as I ducked to avoid a low-hanging limb. "You're hearing an echo? You did hit your head pretty hard." All I could hear was my own labored breathing, her occasional whimpering, and the rustle of the wildlife we disturbed.

She made a noise and those obscenely long lashes of hers blinked away the snowflakes that were clinging to the tips. "No, my name is Echo, not Snow White."

I lifted an eyebrow and let out a low grunt. "Echo? That's different. Is it your real name?" I was used to strippers named Honor and hookers named Roxie, so I knew it was possible for her to go by something else if there was a role she was playing in her life. I was used to everyone having two faces and multiple personalities. Where I was from, you were whoever you had to be in order to survive.

She groaned again and her eyes closed. "You wouldn't believe how often I've had to show my driver's license to prove it's my real name. My parents had a flair for the unusual. My little sister was Xanthe and my little brother is Horatio."

Those were uncommon, but what caught my ear was the *was* when she mentioned her sister. I was good at hearing the things people didn't say. It had kept me alive for a long time in a place that ate the weak for breakfast.

"Your sister pass away? You said she *was* Xanthe." I swore as my boots slipped on the snow and as the leather strap attached to the shotgun dug into my shoulder. I'd been lying on a prison infirmary gurney less than five months ago, losing most of my blood. I still didn't have my full strength back and this trek was taking more out of me than I wanted to admit. I was going to be lucky if I got us both back to the cabin in one piece.

"She died." Her voice was quiet and I could tell the pain laced throughout it had nothing to do with the physical pain she was in from the accident. "Just a few days ago actually." It was still fresh. No wonder she sounded like she was going to start sobbing. "What's your name?"

The question was clearly a way to change the subject and return the focus to me, but that was a question I really didn't want to answer. I looked down at her and saw that she had sharp lines dug into the center of her forehead and along the edges of her mouth. I kind of hoped she passed back out. It was much easier being the new me when she was unconscious.

I blew out a breath and watched the cloud form in the air in front of me. Fuck, it was cold. My ears were starting to sting and I couldn't remember when I'd last felt the tip of my nose.

"The folks around here call me Ben." It was actually a shortened version of my name, but ever since I could walk I'd been a Benny. Dropping the last part was hard but not as hard as convincing the Marshals that I wasn't going to be Carl or Steve when they relocated me. They wanted me to be a different person...and I understood why. But my name was the only thing I had left from my old life and I refused to let it go entirely.

She squinted up at me and then moaned and lifted a hand to her forehead. As she moved I had to adjust my hold on her. I swore again as she started wiggling and grunted when my palm grazed the side of her breast under the thick fabric of my coat. She was stacked, rounded in all the right places and my new resolve to not be an asshole couldn't beat back the fact that I had always been a boob man. She was working with all my favorite attributes and it was classic old me to notice that while she was bleeding all over both of us.

"What flavor of Ben are you? A Benjie, a Benjamin, or maybe a Bernard?" Her voice was getting thready and weak but I could smell smoke from the fire I had started at the cabin earlier in the evening. I sent up some silent thanks that we were both going to be under a roof and warm soon.

I shook my head, which sent snow flying in every direction, and felt my lips twitch, which made my beard move. I always preferred polished to rugged, but the way women eye-fucked me on the regular with the face fuzz made me wonder if I had been missing out on a surefire way to get laid all these years. I liked women...a lot. In fact, that had been one of my biggest complaints about getting dropped in no-man's-land. The pickings were slim, unless I wanted to keep my options limited to tourists and weekend warriors. I didn't mind the hit-it-and-quit-it type of woman; that's what I tended to gravitate toward.

However, now that I was working out how to be the new me, I figured the way I went about spending time with the opposite sex needed to change as well. I needed to be the kind of guy that deserved a woman's attention for more reasons than the fact I had a pretty face, prettier words, and was blessed with a big dick that I knew how to use.

Grunting and pulling my thoughts away from the kinds of women I was going to be fucking in the future, I answered her question about my name. "None of the above. My mom had high hopes for me; she wanted me to be a doctor or a lawyer. She wanted me to do something that would get us both out of the shithole city where we lived, so she named me Benton. She said it sounded sophisticated and classy." Unfortunately for her, I was always much more a Benny than a Benton. I'd barely made it through high school and by the time I graduated, I was already breaking knees and collecting debts for the monster who called all the shots on my streets. I was making enough money to get my mom out of the Point, but she refused to take it, saying it was dirty and she wouldn't make a deal with the devil. I sold my soul the first chance I got and never looked back. At least, I hadn't until I almost died. That was enough to make a man question every move he made that got him to that point...and landed him in the Point.

The Point was kind of like Surrender in the fact you couldn't pinpoint it on a map. It was the nickname for the bad part of the big city I grew up in. It was a place no one wanted to talk about, and very few made it out of in once piece.

The fed that was in charge of my case would lose his mind if he knew I had given this woman my real name, but I figured she had a concussion and was barely conscious so it wouldn't hurt anything. Plus, I wanted her to know me...well, the me that I'd just decided to be. I wanted to see if I could actually pull off being a guy who deserved a shot at getting it right.

"You don't look like a Benton." Her voice was weak and I could see she was struggling to keep her eyes open.

"Oh yeah? What do I look like then?" I was curious and also leery of what her answer would be. I was supposed to be doing my best to fit in here, to make a new life, so if this banged up and barely awake girl could pinpoint that I didn't belong, I was in deep shit.

Her eyelids fluttered and drifted back over those intense sapphire eyes. Her lips moved slightly and on a whispered breath she exhaled, "You look like trouble."

She had no idea how right she was. I snickered at her words and it bled into a sigh of relief when the clearing where my cabin sat came into view. I hugged the woman closer to my chest and to see if she was still coherent asked, "What are you doing out in the middle of nowhere Montana in the middle of winter and after midnight anyways?"

She didn't respond for a long minute so I assumed she was blacked back out. I almost dropped her when she whispered, "I'm looking for someone. I drove up here to find him."

I looked down at her curiously and her eyes were back open. They were so pretty I found myself staring into them and not moving, even though shelter was a mere hundred yards away. "Who are you looking for?"

She blinked up at me and cocked her head to the side like she was trying to decide if I was friend or foe. Foe. I was always foe, but she didn't need to know that.

"MacKenzie. I'm looking for a MacKenzie."

I couldn't stop the laugh that shook out of my chest. I tilted my head back and hooted up at the night sky as I regained my footing and hauled ass toward the door to my cabin.

"Pop-Tart, you're going to have to narrow those search parameters down."

She squinted her eyes at me and wiggled in my grasp, which made us both moan, her in pain, me at the way everything behind my zipper started to tighten and harden. She didn't ask me about the nickname and I was glad. They had been my favorite things to eat when I was a kid. I used to watch and wait for the sweet treat to pop up out of the toaster like it was my reward for making it through the previous day.

"What do you mean? This town is microscopic. How hard can it be to find one man named MacKenzie?"

I laughed again and jiggled the doorknob, sighing as the warmth from the roaring fire immediately hit my icy skin. "This town is tiny but more than half the year-round residents are MacKenzies. Men, women, children…they're all part of the MacKenzie brood. The sheriff is a MacKenzie, the town doctor is a MacKenzie. You can't throw a rock in Surrender without hitting one of them." I tended to avoid them. Most of the men had ties to the military and different clandestine government agencies. They worked to put the kind of people I spent a lifetime doing business with down. I didn't want to be on the wrong side of MacKenzie-style vengeance, which was another reason I knew the Marshals dropped me here. It was easier to keep my nose clean when I was living smack dab in the center of a lion's den.

Those blue eyes widened and then squeezed shut like my words had hit her right in the heart. "You've got to be kidding me."

"Not really a kidding kind of guy." I walked over to my bed, which was still messy from last night, and gently laid her down on it. She went to push herself up into a sitting position but let out a strangled scream that echoed loudly in the small space when she put pressure on that left arm. We were going to have to do something about that shoulder. "Gotta try and get your shoulder back in the socket, Pop-Tart."

She glared up at me and put her other hand on the offending limb. "Do you have any idea how to do that?"

I shrugged and rubbed my still-cold hands together. "I've seen it done a bunch. The place where I'm from had bareknuckle fights every weekend. No rules, no regulations. Bones broke all the time and they often ended up dislocated. It's gonna hurt like a mother, but it'll feel better once it's back where it belongs." I sounded far more confident than I was.

She gazed at me skeptically and sucked her bottom lip between her teeth. She let it go with a pop and asked me, "Where in the hell are you from that bareknuckle fighting on the weekends is a common activity?"

That made me chuckle. "That's a story for another time. Let's do this, okay?"

She slowly nodded and let her good hand drop. She sucked in a breath as soon as I grasped her wrist and I could feel her pulse pounding like a runaway race horse under my fingers. A single tear leaked out of the corner of her eye and for the first time in my adult life, I regretted that I was going to have to purposely cause harm to another person.

"Gonna count to three." She nodded stiffly and sucked in a

breath. I held mine as I told her "One," and then yanked as hard as I could until I felt muscle and bone slide back into the place it belonged. It happened so fast she didn't get the chance to scream and I wasn't surprised at all when she passed back out.

It had been a long time since I had someone as pretty as she was in my bed. Being locked up was not conducive to getting my dick wet, not unless I was up for a little convict-on-convict action...which I was emphatically not. And when I got out, my ass belonged to the feds and they were watching my every move, so the chance to scratch that itch hadn't yet presented itself. I had plans to pounce on the first ski bunny that crossed my path.

After all, wolves ate rabbits for dinner.

There was something different about this girl. Something special. She'd survived a crash that should have killed her and she was fighting through pain, both physical and emotional, that would cripple almost anyone else. Sadly, I knew that the old me wouldn't have stood a chance with someone as strong as her and I knew down to my bones the new me absolutely didn't deserve someone like her.

Chapter 3

Echo

It was still dark when my eyes popped back open. I was disoriented, sore from the top of my head to the soles of my bare feet, and I couldn't move my left arm. I wasn't sure if it was the same night I'd been rescued by the contradictory stranger or if I had been out for too many hours to count on my one working hand.

Groaning, I looked over at my unresponsive shoulder and snorted when I noticed the reason it was immobile was because there was a heavy bag of frozen French fries resting on top of it. After a quick scan of the rest of my aching frame, I noticed that I had a variety of bandages and Band-Aids holding together the places where my skin had torn open and shredded during the accident. Lifting my good hand, I reached up to touch the top of my head in search of the gash that hadn't seemed like it was ever going to stop bleeding, and was pleasantly surprised to find that the blood that had caked and matted my curls together was no longer there. The wound and the area around it had been cleaned. It was still swollen and obviously needed a stitch or two to shut it, but it was no longer bleeding, which I was going to consider a win under the circumstances.

"How you feeling, Pop-Tart?" His voice came from somewhere across the room. I squinted into the dimly lit surroundings until I spotted him hunched down in front of an old potbelly stove, feeding logs into a fire. I could hear it popping and crackling and the sounds were surprisingly soothing. The material of his dark, thermal shirt pulled tight across his broad shoulders and when he glanced over at me again, I was struck by how clear and sharp those fog-colored eyes of his were.

"I feel like I was in a car accident and was lucky to survive it. Did you chop all that wood?" I knew I sounded incredulous, but for the life of me I couldn't picture a guy named Benton, one who wore a ring like that, and clearly cared more about his hair than most women I knew, laboring over something as rustic and old-fashioned as chopping wood for a fire.

A low chuckle rumbled out of his chest and he lifted a dark eyebrow at me. "Maybe. Would it impress you if I told you that I did?"

"Only if I believed it was true. I don't think there's such a thing as executive lumberjacks or corporate woodsmen." I shifted my legs under the thick quilt that was covering me and frowned when I realized my legs were bare and that I had on a pair of thick wool socks that were definitely not mine. "Did you take my clothes off?" The question came out more of a squeak than a defiant burst of outrage.

He rose to his feet with a smooth shift of muscle and crossed his arms over that broad chest that I could tell was distinctly cut with powerful muscle and obviously latent strength. A shiver of unease slithered down my spine as the reality of how isolated we were hit me, right along with the awareness of just how big and capable he seemed to be.

He lifted a shoulder and let it fall in a careless shrug. "I had to. I wanted to make sure that wound on the top of your head was cleaned and flushed out since I don't have anything on hand to close it and the last thing you want is to get a head injury infected. There was no way to wash it and your hair out without drenching you. Don't worry, I behaved myself. When I have a woman in my bed, I like her to have a little more fight in her then you've had since we've met."

I blinked up at the wooden ceiling and lifted my hand to rub my eyes. They felt grainy and dry. "How long have I been out?" I didn't have a recollection of anything after him grabbing my arm and jerking my shoulder back to where it was supposed to go.

"Around twenty-four hours. It's almost the same time as I found you yesterday. I'm running out of frozen shit to put on your shoulder. It's so warm in here, none of it stays cold for very long. Why did you call me an executive lumberjack?" His lips quirked when he asked the question as he moved across the room to a microscopic kitchenette. He'd called it a cabin when he was carrying me through the woods and he wasn't lying. There didn't seem to be much to the space besides four bare walls, a couple of windows, the ancient stove, and the admittedly plush and comfy bed I was currently sprawled across.

"Because you're dressed like you live in the woods but not like you've lived here forever. The clothes are practical but it almost seems like you're wearing a costume. You look good in jeans and flannel but something tells me you would prefer a three-piece suit. One that costs a mint, if that ring you wear is anything to go by." That was a lot of words for a mouth that hadn't had anything to drink in a very long time. I tried to prop myself up on my good arm but my battered body protested immediately. Sighing at the ceiling, I quietly asked, "Would you mind getting me a glass of water? My mouth feels like the Sahara."

I heard a faucet turn on and seconds later the bed dipped on my good side. A glass was held in front of me as I contemplated how I was going to sit up without sending spears of pain throughout my body. Ben solved the predicament by putting his free hand on the center of my back and slowly lifting me up. My shoulder still screamed in protest and the pain made my vision go spotty, but when that subsided, everything else seemed to be nothing more than a low ache and a dull throb.

I stared into those amazing eyes of his and offered up a weak thanks. His lips twitched like he found the entire situation amusing and he gave his dark head a little shake. "No problem. You picked a good day to come crashing down my mountain, Pop-Tart. It was the day I decided to turn over a new leaf."

My eye skimmed over the jagged scar marring his throat. It was impossible to ignore. This close to him, it looked even more brutal and violent. He was also lucky to be alive.

"If things like that happened under your old leaf, I'm thinking it was a good call." I tilted my chin in the direction of his marked throat and he lifted his fingers to touch the vivid reminder that he should probably appreciate every moment he was still breathing.

"Things like this were par for the course under my old leaf, and you're right...I used to wear a very different uniform when I was there." He pushed off the bed and ran a hand over his beard. "I'm trying to convince myself this leaf isn't so bad, but I'm not quite there yet." Bringing obvious truth to his words, he twisted that big, blingy ring on his finger.

I sucked back the water and held out the glass in response when he asked me if I wanted another. "So, where exactly was your old leaf located? That's the second time you mentioned that you weren't from around here originally."

He looked over his shoulder at me and the corners of his mouth pulled down in a frown. He brought me the second glass of water, wandered back over to the kitchen and started rustling his way through one of two rickety-looking cabinets that I assumed stored his provisions. "You want something to eat? It's mostly frozen garbage and a lot of meat but I think there is some soup stashed somewhere in here."

I didn't feel hungry but it had been a long time since I'd put anything in my stomach. "I could probably keep some soup down, if you make it. What I really need is something for the pain in my shoulder. Do you have any Tylenol or Advil?" I really wanted morphine but with my history of addiction and overindulgence, I never hit the hard stuff.

"Let me check the first aid kit. I think I saw some in there when I was digging around for bandages to patch you up. If all else fails, I have a bottle of bourbon that'll do the trick."

I cleared my throat and pushed a wild curl out of my face. I usually wore my unruly locks pulled back, but after everything they'd been through the last couple of days, they were more than likely a wild riot of tangles curls, spinning and spiraling in a million directions all over my head. "I...ugh...I don't actually drink. I won't take anything stronger than Tylenol."

Soup can in hand, he turned to look at me. He blinked slowly and cocked his head to the side. "Is there a story there?"

I wanted to shrug but knew it would feel like a thousand angry bee stings if I did. "There is. One that's not particularly new or original." I lifted my eyebrows at him. "How about you? Are you purposely avoiding telling me where you were before you were here?"

His beard twitched as a grin tugged at his attractively curved mouth. "You're sharp for a chick that just rolled down a mountain." That made me snort out a surprised laugh. "Where I'm from is a shithole of the worst kind, but it was my shithole and I miss it." He turned back to the counter, where there was a single electric burner resting. "It's a bad place, a dangerous place, and I did my fair share making it that way while I was there. That's about all I can say about it."

Well, that was the opposite of reassuring.

I'd always been a girl that liked herself a bad kind of boy. Part of it was because those were the kind of guys that gravitated to my lifestyle choices. I liked to party. I liked to have a good time, and I liked not being questioned about it. Now, as a much more self-aware woman, I knew that I always drifted toward those types of men because it was what was expected of me. My parents never had any faith in me, and somewhere along the line, I'd lost faith in myself. I stopped having expectations and was okay being a user, who in turn was used. But after my best friend died simply because she picked a guy that wasn't all that different than the type I normally picked, I realized I needed to start being the person I really was, rather than the person everyone expected me to be.

I got clean.

There was no more using, of substances or people. I quit cold turkey, took my happy ass to rehab and therapy. I had made great strides toward becoming a better person. I didn't look twice at boys that were going to be trouble and I avoided men that were going to disrupt my self-improvement at all costs.

Until I literally fell into Ben's arms. He was on an entirely different level than any of the guys I'd messed around with before crashing into his life.

He wasn't a bad boy…he was a man that just admitted to being bad. He was dangerous. He was quietly threatening and menacing…even though none of it was directed toward me. I had no problem imagining him doing really bad things in a place he wouldn't give a name to. It made the fact I was alone with him and at a severe disadvantage because of my injury crawl uneasily across my skin.

"How can you miss a place where someone tried to kill you? How can you miss a place so violent?" My voice shook a little bit but he didn't turn around from his task.

"It's all I know." He said it without a hint of remorse or regret. "Have you ever heard the phrase 'absolute power corrupts absolutely'?"

He finally glanced over his shoulder at me and frowned at the expression on my face. I knew I was watching him like he might pounce any second but I couldn't help it. I felt like prey with its paw caught in a trap. "Yeah. I think I've heard something along those lines before."

He nodded and turned back to the pot he was methodically stirring. "It's true. Whatever you've had, whatever you've tried…none of that compares to how instantly and wholly addictive power is. All you need is a little taste, just a hint of it on your tongue, and you're a goner. Soon it's all you can think about. All you want is more and more. Before you know it, you're doing anything, even things that turn your stomach and make your mother disown you to get your hands on more of it." He looked over his shoulder at me once again and I sucked in a breath because his eyes had shifted from the color of clouds to something sharp and deadly. "I don't think your story and mine are so different, Pop-Tart."

I swore under my breath and pushed back my wayward hair. "Mine doesn't have someone angry enough at me to slit my throat, Ben."

I watched as he lifted a hand to that raised and still-healing scar. It was almost like he had to touch it in order to remember that it was there.

He let his hand drop and his eyes practically sliced into me as he emotionlessly told me, "Made a lot of really nasty people mad during my fall from grace and I managed to take a solid handful of them down with me. It was only a matter of time before one of them found a way to make sure I knew just how mad they were. Like I said, par for the course, which is why that new leaf is looking pretty good. I just had to get my head out of my ass and realize it. I've been spending a lot of time feeling sorry for myself lately."

"You have to be accountable for the choices you've made, even the wrong ones." That was something that had been made startlingly clear when I tried to get custody of Hyde and was turned down flat because of my past mistakes. No one else had done those things, only me, but I wasn't suffering from those choices alone.

He turned from the burner and sauntered over with a chipped bowl in his big hands to where I was still taking up the entire bed. The plume of steam coming off the top was very inviting and he suddenly didn't seem as scary tasked with something so domestic and mundane.

He handed me the soup and leaned back to loom over me with his arms crossed over his chest. I blamed the lingering effects of the concussion for the way my gaze drank in the sight of his shirt straining against thick muscle. My mouth watered and it had nothing to do with the yawning emptiness in my stomach.

He was really too attractive to be sequestered out here in the wilderness alone. That seemed like a crime against womankind.

"Being accountable for your actions, that mandate include your sister too?"

I almost dropped the soup all over the bed. The spoon hit the side with a *clink* as I glared up at him. "What are you talking about?" Other than telling him Xanthe had passed away I was sure I hadn't mentioned anything else about her. That was a wound that wasn't going to heal and talking about her was like poking at it with a stick.

His frosty gaze narrowed on me and his chin lifted, giving him an air of superiority that grated. "You messed up. I more than messed up. But your sister…she did something she can't ever take back and it hurt a lot of people. You risked your pretty neck to drive all the way up here, in horrible conditions, to put the blame for her actions on a stranger. Where is her accountability? Where is the knowledge that she was the one responsible for the choice she made? Not you, and definitely not whichever MacKenzie she fixated on." He shrugged. "Denver is usually where you connect when you fly into Montana, so it could have been any one of the brothers. All of whom are happily married and never would have looked at your sister that way as it is."

I sucked in a breath through my teeth and squeezed my eyes shut. He knew too much. Saw too much. I felt like he was peeling back my skin and looking directly at my soul.

"You have no idea what you're talking about." It came out on a whisper that sounded like it had been shredded by razorblades.

He ran his thumb along the edge of his lower lip and watched me without blinking. This was not a man you messed with, and every second spent in his company drove that fact home.

"You talked a lot when you were out. Mumbled about finding your sister in the bathtub. You seemed pretty stuck on the fact that if whichever man your sister was infatuated with had paid her some kind of attention, she wouldn't have taken her own life, but you're sharp, Pop-Tart. You know if it wasn't one of the MacKenzie boys, it would have been someone else. You can't blame anyone for the choice your sister made." He took a step closer to the bed and leaned down so that he could put his palms flat on the mattress. His eyes bored into mine and I could feel the heat of his breath as he quietly stated, "That includes yourself. When your head isn't rattled and your heart isn't hurting, you'll be able to look back and realize you're so fired up to blame one of those boys because it takes the blame you're feeling for not being able to save her off your shoulders." I gasped and scrambled to keep the soup from spilling as he pushed up and off the bed. "Some people are beyond saving. It sucks, but it's true."

I hated him. In that moment, all I wanted was for this man who admitted to doing bad things and being a bad person to be in the ground, and for my sweet, simple sister to still be breathing. It wasn't fair. Even if he'd saved my life.

I handed him the soup bowl, wincing as my shoulder throbbed. "Some people don't deserve to be saved. There is a difference."

Those sinful lips twitched within that forest of dark facial hair again. "There's the fight I was talking about. Now that you're awake, I'm gonna call the doc and the sheriff and see if I can get an ETA on when they can get up here and rescue you."

"Aren't you the one that rescued me?" It was biting and lacking any kind of calm.

He chuckled, but there was no humor in it. "No, I kept you alive, Pop-Tart. There's a difference."

The devil was always in the details, wasn't it?

Chapter 4

Ben

"You sure she's safe up there with you until the roads clear enough to get to her?"

Cooper MacKenzie's voice was gruff and full of suspicion in my ear. I couldn't blame him for being skeptical about my intentions. The Marshals had given him a rundown about all my misdeeds before plunking me down in his backyard. He knew all about the man I used to work for and all about the other men I ratted out to the feds in order to win this sweet spot in WITSEC. He wasn't thrilled to have someone like me in his neck of the woods and he kept his eyes on me. All the MacKenzies did. This was their town and they weren't about to let a dangerous outsider fuck things up.

They were smart.

"She's good. I cleaned her up the best I could, but she's got a gash on her head that needs more medical care than I can give. She dislocated her shoulder and bruised some ribs but that seems to be the worst of it. Obviously, I can't tell if she's got anything internal jacked up but she's responsive and awake, so I'm thinking most of her injuries are superficial."

There was a grunt on the other end of the line. "The car is totaled? Did she say why she was up on the pass in those conditions in the first place? Damn tourists. Always making more work during the winter."

I rubbed my thumb along the side of my mouth and lifted my eyebrows at my bristly patient. She was watching me with narrowed eyes and a tight mouth. She hadn't said a word since I laid out the truth for her. They said it hurt, but I could see in her eyes that in this case the truth killed.

"She was coming up to meet a friend. She thought she could handle the roads because she's from Denver. You might want to have the town tourism board put the fact that Surrender is pretty much Antarctica in the winters on your website and brochures." I kept my voice light but the stern sheriff was in no way amused.

"What friend was she coming to meet? Do I need to get word to someone that she's been located? No one has called in a missing person over the last few days."

I was a good liar, used to spinning words and telling stories to keep my ass out of the fire, but something made me uneasy lying to this cop. This new leaf I was under was starting to get really annoying. Having a conscience and empathy was a real bummer. I was used to being calculating and operating on the assumption that the only person that mattered in the world was me, myself, and I. Having consideration for others sucked and I didn't like the way it scratched across my skin.

"Uh…the friends already know she's okay. She called them on my cell. They aren't local so as soon as the roads clear, they have to head back home. They were just up here for a long weekend and she's going to need to see your brother before she travels. The doc needs to check her head out." Echo narrowed her eyes at me as the untrue words tripped over my tongue. I didn't want any of the MacKenzies to know that they were her target. They would not respond well to having a bee…even one as attractive as she was…in their collective bonnet.

Cooper grunted in my ear again. "I'll tell Thomas. He might be able to get up to the cabin on an ATV before the roads open. There was an emergency here in town last night involving several cars and multiple injuries, so he's had his hands full. I'll tell him to give you a call if he can make it up sooner than expected, Benny." A piece of my soul was soothed when I heard my real name, even though it was said with warning and a clear threat. "You take care of that girl. If she so much as looks at you sideways when I get up there, what the feds can do to you will look like child's play by the time I'm done making your life a living hell. Understood?"

He couldn't see me but that didn't stop me from putting my fingers to my forehead and snapping out a sharp salute. "Aye, aye, captain. I shall remain on my best behavior."

Echo let out a startled-sounding laugh and lifted her fingers to her mouth like she could stem it. I didn't know if she was surprised that she was laughing at me, or surprised she was laughing at all after everything she'd been through recently. Either way, the sound was lyrical, light, and sparked something warm and foreign in the center of my chest. I immediately wanted to do everything I could to make her laugh again.

"Stop being an asshole, Ben, and just take care of the girl. I'll be in touch." The line went dead and I shook my head at his words. I couldn't stop being an asshole. That's what I was. I'd worked hard at it, been conditioned to be the best asshole I could be by the king of all assholes. Those instincts and automatic responses didn't fade away overnight. They were far too ingrained into who I was.

I held the phone out in Echo's direction and asked her, "Do you actually have someone you need to let know you're all right? You're going to be trapped up here for a few days and I'm sure your family is worried about you."

She looked at the phone like it was a venomous snake ready to strike. "No one knows I'm here. I took two weeks off work, packed a bag, and left. My parents haven't spoken to me since I found Xanthe and my little brother is dealing with his grief in his own way." She sighed and shifted under the quilt that still covered her lap. "He lives in Arizona and is kind of a New Age spiritualist. Last I heard, he was on his way to Sedona to seek solace and commune with nature so that he could send Xanthe's soul to the other side peacefully. He doesn't even own a cellphone. The only person I keep in touch with regularly is my best friend's five-year-old son, Hyde. After she died, I helped him find his father, who recently adopted him. He's a good kid, sweet, and his dad is all right too. They both like to check up on me here and there but I didn't tell them I was coming because one, or both, would have tried to talk me out of it."

I let my extended arm drop and blew out a low whistle. "You lost your best friend as well as your sister?"

She blinked, long and slow, and when her eyes lifted to mine, they were glittering with unshed tears. "I did. I buried them six months apart."

I'd never had anyone to lose other than my mother and I hadn't lost her; she let me go when she realized the kind of man I had decided to become. I couldn't say I blamed her, and at the time, I was so drunk on power and privilege that there was no way I could feel the pain of being forgotten and abandoned. Here, looking into this woman's wounded eyes, I could suddenly feel all the sharp and jagged points of that loss tearing apart my soul.

I gave my head a shake to clear it of the foggy memories and new regret. "Well, can I get you anything? It's late and I'm exhausted. I haven't slept since the sound of crunching metal and breaking glass woke me up. I want to make sure you're good, then I'm going to crash."

I put the cell in my back pocket and ran a hand over my hair. There was only one bed in the cabin and she currently had control of it. There was an old army cot outside by the woodpile. It was going to be covered in snow and ungodly uncomfortable, but it would have to do. I'd never been one to sacrifice my own comfort for the needs of someone else, but the new me couldn't imagine asking the poor girl to share the bed and there was no way in hell I was asking her to give it up for the cot.

She lifted a nervous hand and moved some of her very curly hair off of her face. I liked her hair. It was a pretty, rich brown that had a life of its own. It was big, wild, and untamed. I'd liked the way it twisted around my fingers and coiled around my wrist when I was cleaning her up. It was also amazingly soft and silky. Women, where I came from, didn't feel like that. Everything about them was hard, processed, shielded. Nothing was real. Everything about Echo was unvarnished and true.

"I do need something actually." I lifted an eyebrow as she fidgeted nervously, fingers picking at the material of the quilt. "I really have to go to the bathroom and I don't know if I can make it there under my own steam. The room sort of tilts sideways when I move too fast."

It was something simple, something I should have asked her if she needed help with well before now, especially after she guzzled down all that water. I wanted to kick myself for not being better at this whole knight in shining armor thing. I'd spent too long as the dragon, scaring the villagers, and doing the evil king's bidding. Rewiring my brain to work the way any normal man's did was going to take much longer than a day or two, apparently.

"Sure, I'll help you. Just let me know if anything hurts and don't expect five star accommodations. The bathroom is even more barebones than the rest of the cabin." I guess the feds figured anything was a step up from a prison cell, so all I got was the bare minimum.

She pushed the covers off of her long, pale legs and moved to swing them over the side of the bed. All she had on was one of my flannel shirts and a pair of my wool socks. All her clothes were torn, shredded, and covered in blood and mud from the accident. I knew she was naked underneath that thick material and the vision of her shapely, well-toned legs did nothing to help the sudden tightness behind my zipper. She had the prettiest, most milky white skin I had ever seen and right now there was far too much of it on display for my comfort. My fingers tingled with the realization that they were going to be touching it very soon.

She held up her good hand and curled her injured arm protectively across her chest. "Try not to jostle my left side. The shoulder feels better now that it's back in the socket, but it still hurts like a mother when I move it even a little bit."

She curled her fingers around the back of my neck when I lowered myself so I could slide an arm under her bent knees and one around her back. I tried to pick her up as gently and as carefully as possible, but the movement still made her jolt and whimper in pain. She squeezed her eyes shut and pressed her forehead against my throat. I'd never had anyone to take care of before, never had to stop and put anyone else before myself. I had to say, the way satisfaction filled me up and burned through my blood felt almost as heady and potent as the rush I got from my white-knuckled and bloody climb to power in the Point. Normally a naked woman inspired lust and longing; this one had protective and possessive instincts rising up that I'd never felt before.

Almost as if she could read my mind, she asked against my skin, "What did you do before you became an executive lumberjack? How exactly did you make the shithole you call home a bad and dangerous place?"

She needed the words to distract from the obvious pain she was in. I juggled my hold on her soft skin as I opened the squeaking door to the bathroom. Calling it that was a bit of an exaggeration. The thing looked more like what you would find in a campground out in the woods. There was a teeny-tiny shower stall with a rusted showerhead and old camo shower curtain. The showerhead was about two inches lower than where I needed it to be in order to stand up straight while I was in there, so I was getting used to a back ache if I wanted clean hair. The sink was metal and set in an off-balance cabinet that leaned dramatically to the left. I stopped resting my toothbrush on the edge of it after the third time I found it on the floor. The toilet was standard, and probably the only part of the setup that wouldn't make her cringe.

It took some work to get her down and steady on her feet. She was still clutching my shoulders for balance when I answered her question as honestly as I could. "I was a handyman of sorts. I fixed things for the man in charge, no matter what it took, no matter the cost. If he had a problem, fixing that problem started and stopped with me."

She lifted her eyes to mine, white lines of agony stark around the corners. "You were a lackey?" I snorted out a startled laugh and grasped her arm as she worked out how to lower herself down onto the porcelain throne. Once she was situated, she waved me off. "I've got it from here, tough guy."

I gave her a nod and slipped out the door, leaving it slightly cracked so that I could get to her quickly if she passed back out or needed anything.

"I was a lackey. The top lackey, and at the time, I thought it was the shit and that I was the shit. It's funny how quickly your perception changes when your surroundings do. The guy I worked for was bad news, the worst kind of criminal. He had zero morals, zero boundaries, and no scruples. Men, women, children…they were all game to terrorize and manipulate. He had those of us that worked for him brainwashed. He handed us all the money, women, power we could ask for and told us his way was the only way to build the city up. It wasn't until he was gone and we were left with the mess he made that any of us realized we were the ones responsible for tearing the city apart. We were what was wrong with the place."

She let out a little gasp but it didn't sound like one caused by pain, so I stood still outside the door as she asked, "What happened to him? The guy you worked for, is he the one that tried to kill you when your perspective changed?"

I let out a sharp laugh and shook my head. "No, he's dead. He tried to set his own kid up, tried to blackmail him into working for him. When his plan didn't work, he snatched the kid's girlfriend and tried to use her for leverage. As it turned out, the apple didn't fall far from the tree and his kid had no qualms about taking him out. His son is not someone you fuck with and my old boss should have known that." I'd known Bax was bad news and told Novak over and over again he was playing with fire. Shane Baxter was a problem that refused to be solved and Novak paid the ultimate price for not paying attention when I told him that.

I was actually the one that took Bax's girl. I was also the one that smashed her brother's kneecaps in with a tire iron while trying to find her; like I said, anything to try and fix the problem. I reached up to touch the scar at my neck and again wondered if it was one of the soldiers from the cartel I turned on, or one of the henchmen from the human trafficking ring I sold out, or one of the minions that worked for the arms dealer that I burned that had ordered the hit on me while I was locked up. Realistically, I knew it was just as likely that Bax had called in a favor from the days he was locked up for boosting cars. Even though I'd never had one of my own, I knew all the way down to my bones you did not mess with a dangerous man's woman. Not without serious consequences.

I heard water running as she flushed and then washed her hands. The door swung open and I caught her around the waist as she swayed on her feet, much like she had the night she pulled herself out of the wreckage of her car. Her forehead hit my throat again and her working arm wound around my neck as the injured one pressed into my chest. She heaved a deep sigh and her words were warm across my skin when she spoke.

"I'm glad you turned over a new leaf, Ben. The old one sounds pretty terrible."

I ran my hand up and down her back, feeling tension and exhaustion along every lean line of her body. She was about to drop. Without asking, I scooped her up into my arms and started back to the bed.

"The leaf had its moments when it kept the rain out but it definitely isn't a leaf made for everyone." I laid her back down as lightly as I could and bit back a groan of pure male appreciation as my palm skimmed her calves when I helped her get her legs back under the covers. Her skin was as soft as butter and all I wanted to do was keep working my hands up higher and higher until they were under the hem of the too-big shirt that was keeping her covered. "I need to run outside and grab the cot so I can crash. You couldn't pay me enough to sleep on these floors." I hadn't cleaned them in the months I'd been living there and who knew when they'd been mopped before my arrival.

I was getting ready to push off the bed when her fingers curled into the collar of my shirt, balling the cotton up in her fist.

"I don't want to kick you out of your bed, Ben. You've already gone above and beyond the call of duty where this particular damsel in distress is concerned."

I peeled her fingers loose and stood upright. "You aren't kicking me out of my bed, Pop-Tart. I'm willingly giving it to you while you're stuck up here with me." Color me surprised that I actually could be a gentleman on occasion. No one back home would believe it.

She glanced down at the bed then back up at me. Her eyes were so blue it was like drowning in the deepest part of the ocean each time she blinked.

"You don't have to give it up. That's ridiculous. I've been unconscious and at your mercy for who knows how long. If you were going to try anything funny, you would have done it when I couldn't fight back. The bed is big enough to share." She gave me a lopsided smirk and worked herself over to the far side, the side her bad arm was on. "Besides, I normally find myself in bed with the absolutely wrong kind of man. This won't be anything new for me."

Well, wasn't that a kick in the teeth?

I wanted to be the only wrong man she found herself in bed with, but that didn't stop me from pulling back the covers and sliding in next to her. I told myself I would keep my hands to myself and remain on my best behavior.

But like I mentioned...I was a damn good liar.

Chapter 5

Echo

I couldn't get comfortable. I was so tired my entire body felt like it was made of lead, my limbs were too heavy to lift, and my eyes were too tired to stay open. The dull throb in my shoulder, the ache that wouldn't stop, kept me wide awake and shifting restlessly all night long as sleep eluded me. I tried to be as still as I could so that I didn't disturb or accidentally bump into my distractingly attractive bedmate, but it only took a half hour before my restlessness had him rolling out of bed and padding quietly across the small space.

I opened my mouth to apologize for forcing him out of his bed when he was as obviously exhausted as I was, but the words were drowned out by the sound of running water and the clinking of metal on metal as he put a cast-iron pan on top of the stove. He bent to throw a couple more logs into the dwindling fire, making my mouth go dry when he stripped his shirt off as a burst of heat filled the room. I knew he was strong and packing some serious definition under that winter-appropriate clothing. However, there was no being prepared for the pure masculine beauty that was put on display when they were removed. His skin was touched with gold and orange light from the open door of the stove, highlighting thick slabs of muscle and a stomach that looked like it had been chiseled from stone. Every part of him was cut, defined, and sharp. There wasn't an extra ounce of fat on him anywhere, and he had a little dusting of dark chest hair that spread out and arrowed down across that impressive stomach toward the happiest trail I had ever seen.

I wanted to run my fingers over it. I wanted to touch it and stroke it to see if it was as soft as his beard was. The man didn't mess around when it came to product and personal hygiene. His beard was silky and springy and when I was close enough to him to smell it, all I got was hints of coconut and honey. Not to mention, he hadn't showered or been to bed since rescuing me from the crash site and his thick, dark hair was stuck firmly in its trendy style.

"The only thing I can think of to help you get comfortable so we can both sleep is putting some heat on that shoulder. All we have to work with is an old-fashioned heating bag that needs to be filled with hot water. Once this boils, you should be good to go." He bent back down to add more wood to the fire and I had to literally bite my lips to hold in a moan when all the muscles and lines of his back flexed and bunched enticingly. There was something about how unquestionably strong he was, both in mind and body, that called to the broken parts of my heart. He was a man that might bend when he had to, but he would never break. There was something so appealing about that after everything I'd lost recently.

He was also the only person that had gone out of their way to take care of me in as long as I could remember. My entire life had been about taking care of my sister, and taking care of myself. There was never anyone to lean on or rely on…until this confusing and difficult stranger. I wanted to hate him for the way he wielded the truth like a blade, but I couldn't because his care and concern made hating him impossible. The feelings he had churning under my skin were as out of place as he was in this cabin in the woods.

I heaved a sigh and lifted my hand to rub my gritty eyes. "I'm so sorry that I'm being a burden. I'm usually really good at taking care of myself." At least I was, now that I was purposely avoiding the things I used to use to hurt myself.

There was a rustling sound then a volley of swear words that I assumed meant he'd splashed some of the hot water on himself as he was filling the rubbery hot water bottle. Moments later, the soothing heat was resting on my shoulder and some of the pulsing pain ebbed away. I blinked up at him as his fingertips touched my forehead. I held my breath as he moved a curl away from my face with the singularly gentlest touch I'd ever experienced in my life.

Those hands had committed crimes.

Those hands had blood on them.

Those hands had been used to hurt others.

Those hands were dirty in a way that would never wash clean.

I shouldn't want them all over the rest of my body, but I did.

"The morning of your crash, I was looking at myself in the mirror. I was wondering for the umpteenth time why I didn't die when by all accounts I should have. If the kid that sliced my throat had managed to get the blade a little more to the left, just a millimeter or two, I wouldn't be here. He was so close to my jugular that everyone called it a miracle I made it." He brushed his thumb over the arch in my eyebrow and the corners of his mouth lifted up in a grin. "It wasn't a miracle; it was fate. The only reason I survived was so that I could be here to make sure you made it. I was never the one that earned the second chance. You were." He moved away from where he was leaning over me, leaving me breathless and tingling from top to toe. "You lost a lot, Pop-Tart. The only reason I pulled through was to make sure you didn't lose yourself as well." His hands moved to the buckle on his leather belt and he lifted a raven-colored brow at me questioningly. "It's hot as hell in here now with all the added fuel on the fire. I'm stripping down, so if you want to change your mind about sharing the bed, now is the time to speak up."

No way was I going to complain about seeing the rest of him stripped down and touched by the light glow coming from the slats on the stove where the fire was indeed raging and popping furiously.

"It's fine." The words came out higher and breathier than I intended. "I'm exhausted and now that my shoulder isn't hurting as bad, I'll be asleep as soon as I close my eyes."

He grunted in response and the next thing I knew, his jeans hit the floor and he was climbing in the bed next to me, wearing nothing more than a pair of sinfully tight boxer briefs. The rest of him was just as nice as his front and back. He was all long, lean lines and coiled strength that looked even better when it wasn't covered up in clothing. He also had a nasty-looking scar that ran up the length of one of his legs, like he'd had to have reparative surgery at some point in the past…like someone had shattered his kneecap. His body was like a topographical map of violence and brutality. Raised marks and bumps indicating broken bones and long-healed injuries. Even his nose was slightly off center, the only real imperfection on his otherwise remarkable face. I didn't understand how anyone forged out of so much ugliness could be so considerate and kind. Everything about him was out of place and so confusing.

"You said it was a kid that gave you that scar across your throat. It happened recently, didn't it?" I should have been silent, chasing after sleep, but I couldn't stop the curiosity about him and where he had come from. I wanted to know all there was to know about him. It was a very different feeling than I usually had when I found myself in bed with a stranger. In the past, all I wanted to do was forget. With Ben, I wanted to know everything because memories of him were all I was going to have once I got off this mountain and back home.

He was silent for a long moment, clearly deciding how much he could, or would, say. The bed shifted as he bent an arm up behind his head and used the other to stroke his beard. I wanted to knock his fingers away and sink my own into the dark fur. I liked guys with facial hair. I was a Colorado native, that meant finding a nice beard attractive was practically a requirement for any single, straight woman from my state.

I wasn't lying when I told myself that I liked Ben's beard more than most.

"It happened around four months ago. I was locked up. When my old boss went down, the feds scooped up his entire crew on RICO charges. They tried to flip most of us, but didn't get the chance. The old boss did business with the worst kind of people and they weren't going to give any of his lackeys a chance to throw a wrench in their operations. Most of the crew got whacked while they were waiting for their trials or working on making deals. They never got the chance to rat the boss's suppliers out." His fingers moved to the scar on his neck and I couldn't resist the urge to touch anymore. I stretched my hand out and brushed my fingertips along the raised, smooth line along his neck. It felt hot to the touch. I wasn't surprised at all when he dropped the bomb that he was an ex-con. I knew he was dangerous and he'd been disarmingly honest about the man he was before he was an executive lumberjack.

"I was never going to turn on anyone. I knew it was going to mean life in prison, or as long as I lasted, but I'm not a rat." He chuckled into the darkness and wrapped his fingers around my wrist, where my pulse was thundering as I traced that wicked scar over and over again. "I thought I was doing an alright job watching my back. I was in for a couple months, had an in with one of the gangs we did business with on the outside. This kid—and I mean he literally was a child, no more than eighteen—I didn't see him coming. He got me when the guards were doing cell checks and distracted looking for contraband. Filleted me open like I was a fish, with nothing more than a razor blade from a plastic razor. He could have been working for one of the crews that was worried I would turn. He could have been trying to earn his prison cred by taking out a big fish. He might have owed one of the guys I pissed off on the streets a favor. Who knows why he did it, because one way or the other it was coming. The prison doc did his best to save my life but it was the feds who came in and really made sure I didn't kick it. They got me to a hospital and put the best otolaryngologist they could on my case. When I pulled through, they told me I owed them and I couldn't argue. I sang louder and prettier than a choir on Sunday."

I went to pull my fingers away from where his pulse was strong and steady under my touch, but he trapped my fingers in his and I sucked in a breath as he brought them to his lips. He brushed a kiss across the tip of each digit before letting my hand fall so that it was resting on the spot in his chest where his heart was beating.

"How much of that am I not supposed to know?" The words whispered out and disappeared into the darkness.

"All of it." There was humor in his tone. "But I've never been very good at following the rules. If you want to sell me out to the highest bidder you can find, more power to you. As it turns out, I'm pretty fucking hard to take down. I've got more lives than a cat." I'd already wasted more than one of those lives and I wasn't about to squander any more.

I curled my fingers into the warm skin and lulling beat they were resting on. I wanted to hold his heart. I wanted reassurance that it was as strong as it seemed to be.

"I'm lucky I never ended up in jail. I'm even luckier I didn't end up like my best friend. I have a habit for drifting toward things that aren't good for me and a lot of those things could have gone much worse than they did."

He turned his head to look at me and even in the mellow darkness I could make out the sharp edge of his nearly silver gaze. "How long have you been clean?"

I barked out a laugh that had no humor in it. Of course he would be able to spot an ex-addict when she was in bed with him. From the sounds of things, he used to be the reason people like me could feed that kind of habit.

"Almost a year. When Halloran, my friend that got killed, hooked up with her last boyfriend and started making choices that were really dangerous for her kid, it was a wakeup call. That little boy needed someone he could rely on and that someone was me. Plus, my sister moved out of my parents' house finally and in with me. I needed to get my act together for her as well, but in both cases, it was too late. I lost them both while I was sober, so there was no hiding how bad that hurt or drowning out every regret and mistake I made along the way." I had been tempted…so tempted to go back to my old ways. I could numb everything eating me up inside with a single hit, but then I'd need another and another. It was an endless cycle and I knew the only way to deal with the pain was to confront it head-on. I couldn't be afraid of it; I had to face it.

He rolled over onto his side and stretched an arm out so that it was resting across my middle. His fingers curled around the side of my hip and dug into the gentle swell of flesh. My hand ended up curled around his ribs, trapped by his weight and the mattress underneath.

"Tell me about your sister. Tell me why you think it was your job to save her and avenge her. Tell me why you would risk everything for her."

I tilted my head on the pillow so we were looking at each other. I exhaled and he parted his lips and breathed the sound in. It was probably the most intimate act I'd ever been a part of.

"She was my little sister. Isn't that enough?" I'd always done my best to take care of her even when I wasn't taking care of myself.

"It's enough…for most people. But for you to feel like you had to come all this way on the limited information you had when you are clearly a smart and capable woman, I'm sure there is more to it than familial obligation."

He thought I was smart and capable.

If I could have moved, I would have rolled toward him and crawled all over that big body, leaving no inch of taut, toned skin untouched. He had no idea how much those words meant to me. How hard I had worked to be that woman.

"Xanthe was always a little different; hell, we all were. Horatio was born to find peace and harmony in everything, Xanthe was born to make everyone smile, and I was created to bring chaos and disruption. My brother and sister were always easy kids. Warm, loving, kind. I was none of those things and my parents never let me forget it. As my brother and sister got older, Horatio came into his own, found a balance between his ideals and the real world, but Xanthe didn't. She lived in a fantasy world where everyone was as nice as she was, where no one would ever hurt anyone else. It made her a target."

Without realizing it, my whole body tightened and tensed.

"Men took advantage of her because she was pretty and sweet. She didn't understand boundaries and that what she was giving away, she wouldn't get back. She handed her heart over to whoever smiled at her and was crushed when she figured out they weren't interested in forever. She went from as high as anyone could be, to the lowest of the low in the blink of an eye. Once I got my head out of my ass and focused on what was happening around me, I started looking into what could cause those kind of mood swings. She'd always been delicate, fragile, but my parents wrote it off as nothing more than her being temperamental." I inhaled a sharp breath through my nose and dug my fingers into his side as memories rose up and threatened to choke me.

"She cut herself. All through high school, she took razor blades to her skin. She bounced from activity to activity and tended to be even more promiscuous than I was. I'm pretty sure if we had taken her to a doctor, if my parents hadn't been so willing to turn a blind eye to how dangerous her behavior was, she would have been diagnosed as bipolar. She needed more help than I could give her. When she moved in with me, I thought I could convince her to go, but just like me, she spent her childhood hearing she was one thing and that's what she believed. She wasn't sick; she was special."

"How did she end up in the path of one of the MacKenzies?" His voice was low and soothing. It settled some of my jangling nerves.

"She worked at one of the coffee shops at the airport. She came home one day and told me she'd met the man of her dreams. Granted, she said that a lot, so initially I ignored her. If I had been paying attention, I would have noticed she was becoming manic, focused, obsessed in a scary way. She didn't even know the guy's first name, but he smiled at her and she was convinced he was in the airport so often just to see her. She had a wedding dress picked out and names for the kids ready to go." I sighed and wiggled my hand free from his weight so I could push on my tired eyes. "She followed him one day to his gate and came home so she could start researching everything about Surrender. It sounds so crazy when I talk about it. I should have been able to stop it."

He offered up a grunt in response that gave no indication as to what he was thinking.

"He came back through the airport after missing a few months and he was wearing a wedding ring. God, Xanthe was inconsolable after that. She was crushed. She cried for weeks, stopped going to work, quit eating and bathing. I tried to talk to her, tried to convince her to let me help, but she totally shut down. My parents told me to ride it out, that it was just a phase, but I knew better. She was off, she was going down, she was slipping off the edge, and I wasn't fast enough or strong enough to catch her. I should have forced her to get help, but I was scared she would resent me, hate me, the way my parents always have. I didn't want to lose her; she was the only one that never let me get totally lost. I always had to find my way back to take care of her. But I lost her anyway. I came home from work one day and found her in the bathtub. She took a handful of sleeping pills and drifted away."

I had to wipe tears away and clear my throat before I could go on.

"I just wanted to tell the guy, the one she was so stuck on, that hearts really can break and when they do, there is no fixing them. I have no clue if he could even pick Xanthe out of a lineup, but he mattered so much to her. You're right. I didn't think it through when I headed up here. I wanted some kind of closure but it isn't going to come from a stranger that probably doesn't even know who my sister is."

My hair moved as he moved closer to me, curling an arm above my head and wrapping his warmth around me. "If you didn't have a busted wing, I would snuggle up on you, Pop-Tart."

I let out a surprised laugh and smiled into the darkness. "If it didn't hurt to move, I would let you." I wanted to rub against that broad chest and press into all the places where he was hard to my soft. For a dangerous man, he made me feel safer than I ever had before.

"For what it's worth, when those MacKenzies fall, they fall hard. Love didn't come easy for them, so they tend be a pretty fierce lot when they get their hands on it. I doubt whichever one it was intentionally did anything to lead your sister on. It was just luck of the draw."

My cheek pressed into his fuzzy chin and I sighed as I was surrounded in the sweet scent of honey. "How do you know so much about them if you're new in town and isolated all the way out here?"

He shrugged and it moved his arm up higher so that my breast was pressing into the inflexible hardness of his bicep. I wasn't nearly as tired as I had been a moment before. My nipples pulled tight and suddenly it was an ache between my legs that was distracting me instead of the one in my shoulder.

"I told you it's a small town and they rule the roost. They're kind of legends around here, so everyone talks. Plus, the feds filled me in. I think they were worried I might accidentally try and score with one of the wives and if I did that, there wouldn't be a surgeon in the country that could save me." He let out a yawn and blinked his eyes at me. On the last blink, they stayed shut and he yawned again.

I was all hot and bothered and he was ready to pass out. It was probably for the best. I was already out of my depths with this guy; if I got any deeper, I would drown. "Goodnight, Ben."

There was no response other than a little breath. I reached up and touched his scar again. He was wrong about not deserving another chance and I was wrong about some people, him included, not being worthy of being saved.

Chapter 6

Ben

I woke up wrapped up in the scent of warm woman with my hands buried in what felt like an endless amount of silky hair. There were curls for days and they were the softest thing I had ever felt. I had a hard-on that was so rigid and stiff it hurt to breathe and at some point in the night, I'd moved so that every inch of my uncovered skin was pressed against hers. One of my legs had wedged between hers, taking the only thing covering her up with it. I could feel the softness of her skin and the gentle heat radiating from her velvety center. I hadn't been this close to a woman in a long time and all my favorite parts of being in bed with one hit me like a ton of bricks. I'd had too much on my plate to worry about the lack of action in my love life as of late, but with Echo mostly naked, the curves of her perfectly rounded backside cradling an erection that felt like it was hard enough to hammer nails, everything I was missing ripped its way through me. I never bothered to *know* the women I usually went to bed with and they were never that interested in knowing anything about me beyond my reputation. I felt a connection to Echo. One that was born from saving her life and in turn, feeling like she might have saved mine.

The thing was, I'd never been this close to a woman that I actually gave a shit about. It felt different. It felt heavy in my gut and significant as it wound its way through my thoughts. It was the only time my heart was throbbing and pulsating with as much intensity as my dick was.

I blew out a breath that moved her hair and had her shifting her weight more fully into me. Her legs twitched and rubbed against mine as her body slowly stiffened and tightened with wakefulness. Her ass moved against the front of me and my cock went even harder, which I couldn't believe was possible. I untangled my hands from her wild hair and rolled onto my back with a groan that was torn from my soul. If it was possible to die of repressed want and desire, I was going to be a dead man by the time she found her way off my mountain. Need clawed hungrily and furiously at my insides, which meant I needed to get out of this bed and put some much-needed space between us before I reverted back to my old ways, which involved me taking advantage of both the girl and the situation we were in.

I threw myself out of the bed and took a minute to stretch my arms up over my head, spine cracking. Without a doubt my hair was sticking up all over my head from the product that I hadn't bothered to wash out the night before, but that didn't stop Echo's ocean-blue eyes rolling over me with an intensity I could feel. I scratched my beard and ran a hand over my chest. Her eyes tracked the motion and her legs twitched under the covers. Her tongue darted out and slicked across the full curve of her lower lip, leaving a wet trail I wanted to taste more than I wanted my next breath.

"I'm gonna jump in the shower and then see if I can scare up something for breakfast even though it's closer to lunchtime. I bet the doc makes his way up here sometime today or tomorrow to check you out and if you're cleared to travel, he'll probably take you with him down the mountain and into Surrender. I want to hike out to the accident site and see if I can find your stuff that was thrown out of the car when it flipped. You'll need your ID to get on a plane home."

Her chest shuddered with a sigh and her eyes widened a little when I mentioned the word "home."

She forced her way into a sitting position, the big shirt that she was swimming in falling to cover all the parts of her that were the most distracting. I liked that she wasn't shy or insecure about the way she looked. She didn't need to be; she was beautiful and every kind of temptation I wasn't used to denying myself.

She rolled her shoulders and winced when her bad one lifted, but other than her eyebrows pinching together, she didn't seem to be in too much pain. "Before you tackle that mission, do you think you could help me clean up as well?" She lifted her good arm over her head and gave herself a sniff. I could have told her she smelled just fine, like pine and snow from when she was crawling around on the ground. There was still residual blood trapped at the roots of her hair near that wound that I was sure she was ready to wash away. "I think I can stand up without falling over today. My shoulder still feels like someone is jabbing a hot poker through it, but the pain doesn't make me want to throw up anymore. That water bottle helped."

The idea of her naked and wet with so little space between me and her lusciously curved body made my mouth water and my cock jerk. I growled without meaning to and shook my head to clear the very X-rated and illicit thoughts circling my brain. Without thinking about how she would react, I reached down and adjusted the situation brewing in my boxer briefs. Her eyes widened and she made an audible noise low in her throat. The tension between the two of us was palpable and it was risky.

She wasn't supposed to be here and she wasn't supposed to know who I was, the new me or the old me. I'd given her too much because I was selfish and tired of pretending to be someone I wasn't. I'd put her in danger at the same time I'd done my best to stop her from doing something she would regret. I wasn't about to add myself to the list of mistakes and rash decisions she was making in order to distract herself from her grief.

I dropped my arms to my sides and dipped my chin down in reluctant agreement. It was going to be torture, but I'd survived much worse. Plus, if I got fifteen minutes in the shower to work myself over and take the edge off, I wouldn't feel so much like an animal ready to pounce and feed on its captured prey. "Yeah, I'll hang around and make sure you don't drown or fall over and hit your head. I'll stoke the fire again and get more water boiling so you can put the heating pad back on while I clean up."

She nodded and shifted her gaze away from the prominent bulge that was in desperate need of her attention. "That works."

I took care of all the things I told her I was going to and made my way into the minuscule bathroom. I couldn't strip fast enough and the trickle of warm water that came out of the showerhead was hardly enough to wash away the rampant longing that was crawling all over me. It also wasn't enough to melt away the coiled tension that spread across the span of my shoulders and along the length of my spine.

The only thing that helped was the pressure of my fist wrapped around the steel rod that was pointing up directly at my stomach. I closed my eyes and pretended it was something else tight and slick that was wrapped around my cock…pretended it was *someone* else.

I could see the bright blue of her eyes blazing.

I could see the elegant curve of her hips and the enticing roundness of her breasts.

I could see the long sweep of her endless legs.

I could feel the satin texture of her skin and the silken tangle of her hair.

It was so vivid and real that it didn't take long for pleasure to unfurl and shoot up my spine. My entire body vibrated with the release and my head fell forward as the sharp lines of tension finally loosened the hold they had on my neck. I gave a deep sigh of relief and dropped my forehead to the tiles in front of me so I could get my head under the water. Now that my lust was semi in check, I needed to get my mind out from between Echo's legs and back on the task of making sure she was healthy and whole when Thomas MacKenzie showed up to check on her.

I stepped out of the basin and wrapped a threadbare towel around my waist. I only had a couple of them on hand and I wasn't sure if any of them were exactly clean. Back in the day, I used to wine and dine women with gourmet meals and nights spent in luxury hotels. I finally met a woman I liked, one that could matter if the situation was different, and I couldn't even offer her a clean towel.

Shaking my head at the ridiculousness of the situation, I sent water droplets flying everywhere. I was lifting a hand to wipe away the condensation on the mirror so I could run a comb through my hair when there was a tap on the door. Leaning over, I pushed it open and was met with a red-faced and anxiously waiting Echo.

She let out a strangled-sounding gasp when the door swung open and the hand she had used to knock went to her throat. Her long lashes swept down as her eyes dropped to my still wet chest. I could feel their impact like it was touching my skin. She watched water droplets roll across my abs until they disappeared underneath the towel at my waist without blinking.

"Uhh…well, the walls are thin." She went scarlet and jerked her gaze up to mine. "I heard the water turn off...and umm...well, when you were finished."

My eyebrows shot up to my hairline and a chuckle rumbled out of my chest at her stuttering admission. She was telling me she had listened to me jerk off while thinking about her. A better man would be embarrassed and apologize. I wasn't even a good man, so there was no way that was happening.

I shrugged my shoulders at her and pointed at my once again stirring cock. Anytime I was close enough to breathe the same air as her, I seemed to get hard. "You saw what I was dealing with when I climbed out of bed. It wasn't going to go away on its own." I had a beast that was used to being fed regularly, and lately I'd been starving it. "Give me a minute and you can get in here."

"Well...I uh...kind of figured since you were already in here and wet, I would just jump in behind you so you don't have to worry about changing again after you help me wash my hair. That shower is the smallest thing I've ever seen; there is no way you can help me without getting soaked." She tilted her head back so she was looking in my eyes and when she smiled at me, it took every ounce of self-control I had not to grab her, lift her up on the counter, and make a permanent place for myself between her legs. "I figured this was more practical."

What it was, was sweet agony. If the feds wanted to get me to talk, they should have sent her in with her calculating eyes and alluring body. I would have rolled over in a hot second and given them whatever they wanted if it meant I got the chance to touch her, put my mouth on her.

"It's a lot of things, Pop-Tart, but practical isn't one of them." I inclined my head into the narrow, muggy room and gave her enough space to slide in around me. I leaned against the sink and gave her a challenging smirk. "I think this is the first time I've ever gotten a woman naked in order to clean her up instead of getting her dirty." I circled a finger in the air in front of her. "Strip."

She automatically moved to follow my direction, which meant my dick went rock hard. I liked a woman with fight, but I liked it even more when that fight faded to obedience. She let out a yelp when she moved her bad arm without thinking. I swore when she had to blink away tears of pain as she let the limb drop back to her side.

I took a step toward her, reaching for the hem of my shirt that covered her to mid-thigh. "I forgot for a second that you can't handle the basics right now, which is the only reason I'm here. I'll take care of you, promise." I skimmed the thick fabric over her curves and off over her head, my lungs seizing and my heart stopping when I was face to face with her full breasts, perfectly pink nipples, and bare center. She was a stunner; all that white skin that looked like porcelain contrasted so vividly against her dark hair. If I was the prince, there was no way a simple kiss would ever do if Snow White looked like her. It was impossible to resist the urge to touch, to taste.

She didn't try and cover up, but a pretty flush did find its way across her chest and up her throat. She turned on her foot and climbed into the shower I had just vacated. I leaned against the rickety vanity once again and watched her as she cranked on the water without closing the shower curtain. She was short enough that the stream hit her on the top of the head when it came on, making her jump as water touched her wound. Immediately, rivulets of rosy colored water started to track over her skin as her hair went slick, the curls heavy with moisture.

I waited for her to tell me to go, to insist. I waited for her to look at me and tell me she was fine and would call if she needed me. I kept my eyes glued to her sexy shimmy as she moved her head from side to side in order to make sure she washed away the last of her accident. I knew I should go, but I was rooted in place and it was going to take more than a conscience I didn't have to make me move.

She grabbed my shampoo bottle and held it out to me, blinking water out of her eyes. "Can you squirt this in my hand? I think I can scrub okay with one hand, but I don't think I can get it out of the bottle."

Jesus. She had no sense of self-preservation. She wasn't just pulling the wolf's tail; she was waving a raw steak in front of its giant teeth and exposed claws. If I got close enough to touch, that was exactly what was going to happen. I only had so much self-control and the cords were stretched as thin as they had ever been.

Uncrossing my arms, I pushed off the sink and closed the distance between us. I took the shampoo out of her hand and emptied the viscous liquid into my own palm. "Turn around and I'll do it for you. I don't want you to aggravate that wound. It still looks pretty ugly."

Again, she followed my order without complaint. I had a hungry growl working its way up through my chest but I managed to bite it back. I sank my hands into her hair and started to work up a lather. I lightly skimmed my fingers over her scalp and slipped her curls through my palms. I'd never had a gentle bone in my body but suddenly I was learning I could be all kinds of soft and tender when I needed to be. The fingers on her injured side twitched as she lifted her good arm in front of her, her hand skimming across the swell of her breasts. My brain short-circuited and forgot everything it knew before her when she caught one of those very pink, very pointed nipples between her fingers and gave a little tug.

My stomach tightened, my cock kicked under the towel, and my thighs locked.

She tilted her head to the side and gave me a sultry, searching look as I worked my hands down the length of her hair. "You were thinking about me while you were in here, weren't you? I heard you say my name." She let go of the hold she had on her breast and her long, tapered fingers danced over the smooth skin of her stomach as she watched me and waited for an answer.

I guided the water over her hair with my hands and chased the suds down the line of her back and over the curve of her backside. She sucked in a breath at the blatant caress, but her eyes held mine, waiting for an answer.

"I was thinking about sex with you while I was in here. I was thinking how good you would feel, how sweet you would taste. It was the two of us together that got me off, not the idea of a hot, naked girl who is pretty much at my mercy." That was something that would have gotten me off in the past, but with her, I wanted more.

I wanted her to want me for more than the fact that she owed me something.

"Oh." Her teeth bit into her bottom lip at my words and the hand that was circling her belly button dipped into that valley between her legs that I was pretty sure was where heaven resided. "I feel hot. I feel wet, slippery, and slick." Her eyes blazed, bluer than anything had the right to be, lit with an inner fire I wanted to touch. "I also feel empty. There is an ache here, a throb that matches every beat of my heart."

I watched, still as stone, breathing like I was running a race as her fingers swirled and skipped through glistening folds. She was pink all over, soft as a flower petal, but there was an edge there, something hard and sharp that I liked the most. She wasn't scared of me, of what I could do to her, and that reckless confidence called to something inside.

"Echo." I barked her name as I grabbed her by her good shoulder and turned her so that her back was to the tiled wall and her little show was on full display in front of me. The water ran between the two of us, trickling over her fingers as she alternated between rubbing them over her distended clit and slipping them into all the secret places I wanted inside of. Her skin pebbled up under the weight of my gaze and her chest started to heave as she watched my reaction.

I was about to step in to her, ready to take her mouth with mine and replace her slick and shining fingers with my own, when she suddenly pulled her hand away and lifted it to my slightly parted lips. She smelled like sex and satisfaction. I circled her wrist as she traced the ridge of my bottom lip with her wet fingers.

"You'll have to tell me how I taste, but if I had to wager a guess, I would put my money on turned the fuck on." She lifted her eyebrows up at me and shifted her weight so that her legs were parted in invitation. "Do I taste ready, Ben?"

I sucked her fingers into my mouth and swirled my tongue around each and every one of the slender, delicate digits. I licked between them and dropped a kiss on the center of her palm. She curled her hand around the wet mark I left, like it was something she was going to hold onto forever, and stared up at me as I leaned into her and dropped my mouth down to touch hers.

"You taste perfect, Pop-Tart, but I need another bite to make sure." I kissed her hard, pressing her back into the wall as she gasped into my mouth. I twisted my tongue with hers, gave her the edge of my teeth, and put my hands on her waist so that I could grind my demanding erection into her soft middle. All my senses were overrun by her, her taste, her scent, the tangle of her hair across her pale shoulders, the noises she made in her throat as I took her mouth over and over again. She became the only thing that mattered.

I ground my hips into hers before pulling back and dropping to my knees in front of her. The now icy water coming from the showerhead hit me, but it wasn't enough to cool the fire burning under my skin. I pulled her hips toward my face, grabbed one of her long legs and propped it on my shoulder, gazing up at her as I ran my thumb in circles over the inside of her thigh. I was waiting for her to be the voice of reason, to get us back on the path to sanity and safety, but all she did was put her good hand into the longer top part of my hair and tug. She wasn't going to be smart about this and I didn't have the willpower to protect her from either of us anymore.

I ate her up. My tongue and teeth attacked her wet and welcoming center. She did taste ready, but more than that, she tasted like some kind of sweet salvation. She was clean and untainted, not part of the grit and grime that had spawned me. She was something better, the promise of what could be, and I couldn't get enough of the way that brightness burst across my tongue.

I licked her, sucked her clit in between my teeth, and tortured the little nub with endless flicks from the tip of my tongue. I grazed my teeth across the quivering flesh and let my fingers sink into the greedy heat of her body. She was empty and I was the only one that could fill her up. Her body quaked and shuddered around my fingers, coating them in liquid desire and warm anticipation. Every pulse pulled me in deeper. Every moan she let slip out made me focus on bringing her to the ultimate level of pleasure. I forgot that she was hurt. I forgot that this was an impossible situation. I ignored the fact that I didn't deserve to be the man that was making her feel this good. The only thing I focused on was making sure that no matter what happened when we left this shower, she would never be able to forget this…I would always be with her.

She mumbled my name and pulled on my hair as she undulated against my face. My beard was going to leave red marks on those milky white thighs and I kind of loved that. I was also going to have her pleasure, wet and noticeable, in my facial hair when I finally let her go. It was all so primal. It was the way two people that had nothing left to lose marked one another, clearly, obviously, in ways that were impossible to ignore.

I growled into her, rubbing my chin against her tender skin. She let out a strangled scream and pulled on my hair hard enough that it hurt. I could feel her body getting loose around my fingers, so I let go of her clit with one last tap of my tongue and pulled her up higher, tilting her farther back so that I could replace my plunging fingers with my tongue. I wanted to taste what I did to her, wanted her orgasm on my tongue. I fucked her with my mouth the way my aching dick was dying to do and she broke apart in my hands.

It was the most beautiful thing I had ever seen.

I would gladly take another razor across my throat if it meant the universe was going to throw me in this woman's path and give me the honor of making her shatter. I immediately wanted to do it again and again. I wanted to watch her come while she was straddling me and riding me until I couldn't breathe. I wanted to watch her explode when I had her bent over, that luscious ass in the air as my hips pounded into hers. I wanted to cover her from head to toe as I slid inside of her, eye to eye, heartbeat to heartbeat. I wanted to take her, own her, fill her in every way a man could possess a woman and then, I wanted to start all over again and work my way back down the list.

She was more addictive than power had been, which was why I kissed her low on her belly, rose to my feet, pushed her hair off her face where it clung because of the water. I gruffly reminded her, "I told you I would take care of you." I couldn't get wrapped up in someone I couldn't have. She was going. I was staying, and the last time I got a taste of something I wanted as badly as I wanted her, I'd ruined more lives than I could count. Even if I was willing to go down in flames, I refused to take her with me.

She looked at me in confusion, her eyes drifting down to my painfully hard erection. "What about you?"

I shook my head and stepped back, turning so I could make my escape like a total coward.

"I told you the only reason I'm here is for you, Pop-Tart. Guys like me don't deserve second chances. I'm gonna find something to feed us and then head out. I'm going to leave my cell with you in case the doc calls."

The look in her eyes as before I turned to walk away was one I was achingly familiar with. I'd seen it in my mom's eyes when she told me she didn't ever want anything to do with me again.

It was heartbreak and disappointment, warring for space.

Chapter 7

Echo

I was usually the one that beat a hasty retreat after getting off and coming down. Once I had what I was after, I couldn't get out the door fast enough. Typically, a cloud of shame and regret followed in my wake as I told myself once again, "You should do better."

I liked sex. However, I very rarely liked the men I had it with. They were a means to an end, a tool used to get something I wanted, and then forgotten once I got it. I didn't bother to invest time or energy into getting to know them because I never intended to stick around.

The truth was I was more intimately acquainted with Ben than any other man I'd been with. I knew more about him and he knew more about me than anyone else that had crossed my path in a very long time. Sure, part of that was the fact it was just the two of us out here in the middle of nowhere with no way to get out, but it was more than that. I felt like I understood him. I had a solid grasp on the regret and recrimination that hounded him and made his gray eyes lethally sharp. I lived in that same place of trying to figure out why I was the one that was spared when my sister had such a better, sweeter, softer soul. I understood the need to feed a habit you felt like you couldn't control, even if the pursuit of that thing hurt the people around you. The things he struggled with were scattered on ground I'd traveled a lot in my life and I really wanted to tell him I could show him the way to the place where the path started to go downhill. It would be so much easier for him to find his way if he let me guide him.

But I never got the chance to tell him anything, because after giving me the best orgasm I'd ever had in my life, he disappeared, leaving me weak-kneed and shaking in the freezing cold water still pouring into the shower. By the time I rinsed the rest of my body off and went in search of something clean to wear, the cabin smelled like bacon and eggs but Ben was long gone. He'd left breakfast and a clean shirt, along with a way too-big pair of track pants, but there was no Ben.

I wanted to yell at him, to demand an answer as to how he could walk away from me, walk away from us. I wanted an apology for him so selfishly taking that impressive erection that he'd been taunting me with for hours upon hours, the erection that was rightfully mine, away. It was mine to touch. It was mine to taste. It was mine to savor and satisfy. I was angry that he wound me up, set me off, and let me fall without sticking around to catch me.

I knew he wanted me. The evidence was obvious. So was the fact that he couldn't figure out a way to keep me once he had me. In the end, he decided to give me what I wanted, to take care of me like he had since the day he kept me from face planting in the snow. He denied himself something that was all his for the taking to protect us both from getting any deeper in when we both knew this was our only moment. There was no assurance we would have tomorrow or even tonight; all we were guaranteed were the stolen minutes surrounding us right now. There was no real world intrusions, no harsh light of reality here, even though he tried to force it on me. He did his best to remind me that he was a man that wasn't any good for me off of this mountain and out in the reality of my day-to-day and because he did that, I totally disagreed with him about being worthy of a second chance. He didn't want to be a mistake. But I wanted him to be a memory I would hold onto forever. I wanted my time with him to be the thing I held onto when I got lost and felt like I was alone.

We were two halves of a whole, opposite sides of the same coin, two people cut from the same tattered and torn fabric. His ugliness didn't scare me; it called to my own and made it seem less harsh and unforgiving by comparison. He would never judge me, because he was a man that was too busy judging himself.

I bit into a piece of the bacon he'd left and wandered around the minuscule cabin looking for anything personal or private that would give me an insight into the mystery man that had turned my life upside down and saved me from more than myself.

There was nothing.

Not a single thing.

No pictures or knick-knacks.

No paperwork or documents.

No keepsakes or memorabilia.

All I found was a closet full of mountain man clothing and a jewelry box with a Patek Philippe watch in it. I almost dropped the damn thing, which would have been equal to tossing over a hundred grand on the floor. The watch was so out of place next to the worn denim and heavy flannel that again, I wondered who this man had been before. He was such a complicated mix of ostentatious and simple.

I was tucking the outrageously expensive watch back in its hiding place when the cell phone Ben had left behind jangled and vibrated on the counter. He'd mentioned the town doctor was going to call and try and make his way up to the cabin to give me the all clear to travel, but it was an intrusion into my newfound sanctuary that came much sooner than I anticipated. I moved across the room as quickly as I could, making me breathless when I answered the call.

"Hello." I trapped the phone between my ear and good shoulder as I leaned on the edge of the counter and stared at the door, willing Ben to walk through it and finish what I'd started in the shower.

"Is this Echo Hemsley? My brother Cooper called me yesterday and said you were stranded up on the mountain with a pretty serious set of injuries." His voice was deep and smooth. I wasn't even in the same room with him and I could tell he had a good bedside manner.

"I got pretty banged up when the SUV rolled. I've got a nasty cut on the top of my head so I'm sure I ended up with a mild concussion." I moved my shoulder and let out a wheeze of discomfort. "I also dislocated my shoulder, but Ben, the guy who found me, put it back in place and has been making sure I keep ice and heat on it. I think it's about as good as it's going to get until it heals up."

He muttered something I didn't quite hear and asked, "Are you nauseated at all, out of balance? Do you feel more sleepy than usual or have any ringing in your ears?"

The questions came so quickly that it took me a minute to work through them all in my head. "The first night and into the second day it was a yes to all of that, but I slept normally last night and feel mostly normal today, except for a slight headache and my shoulder hurting like a bitch."

He grunted and I heard the scratch of pen across paper. "Do you feel you need emergency medical care, Ms. Hemsley? I'm the only doctor in Surrender and while I would like a chance to check you out, I would prefer doing it when I can get to you in a vehicle and bring you back to town with me. I would only put someone with all the symptoms of a concussion on the back of an ATV in a true emergency situation. Not to mention, the ride would be incredibly bumpy and miserable on that shoulder."

I snorted out a laugh and shook out my drying curls. "If I didn't die the night of the crash, I'm not going to die now. I think I'll be fine until you can make your way up here in a real car."

"Good. The highway is supposed to open up sometime this evening and I made sure to keep my morning clear tomorrow, just in case. I'll head up the mountain and check you out, then bring you back to Surrender so we can work on a way to get you home."

If Ben found my bag and my purse, it shouldn't be that hard to get me back to Denver. If he didn't, I was going to be in a bind. I didn't have any other form of ID than my driver's license, so there would be no renting a car or getting on a plane if that was lost to the Montana winter. As much as I hated it, I was going to have to call Zeb Fuller, Hyde's dad, and ask him to come and get me because there was no way I was riding a Greyhound through the mountains for hours on end. Just the thought of all those switchbacks made my tummy tighten.

"Sounds like a plan. I would call when you're on your way. Ben doesn't seem too fond of trespassers and likes to greet visitors with the business end of a shotgun."

There was a chuckle on the other end of the phone. "Sounds like he's finally starting to fit in around here. See you in the morning, Echo."

The line went dead just as the door swung open, revealing a panting and soggy-looking Ben. His dark hair had glittering white flakes of snow clinging to it and his off-center nose was tipped red. He kicked the door closed with his boot and I gasped in shock when he dropped my chevron-striped weekender on the floor by his feet. It was filthy, covered in all manner of dirt and debris, but the zipper was still closed and it didn't appear to have any holes in it. I was excited at the prospect of putting on my own clothes and a pair of underwear, but none of that helped me get home.

"No purse?"

His steely gaze tracked my movements as I started toward the bag. "It was a mess. It's been snowing the last couple hours, so it was hard to find anything. The only reason I found this was because I tripped over it."

I sighed but managed a weak smile. "That's fine. You didn't have to go tromping through the woods for this in the first place. I appreciate the effort even if it means I'll have to get creative getting home." I bit down on my lower lip and looked at him from under my eyelashes. "The doctor called. He's coming up in the morning to look me over and take me into town."

"You won't have to get too creative." He reached behind him and pulled a familiar-looking wallet out of his back pocket. Now, it looked like it had seen better days. The leather was torn, half of it looked like it was missing and it was stained with lord only knew. But I could see my driver's license and my credit cards were still in the remaining slots. "I dug around in the car and found this wedged under the back seat."

I gasped at him, jaw dropping open in disbelief. Not at the fact he'd found my ID, but at the fact he had risked his neck crawling around in the demolished SUV. I took the last few steps that separated us and snatched the tattered leather out of his hand, tossing it on the floor next to my bag. "Are you insane? What were you thinking messing with that car? It could have shifted and slid the rest of the way down the mountain. You would have gone with it." I was practically screaming at him but I couldn't pull it back. I worried about him, scared that he was wasting what little time we had left on foolish tasks so he didn't have to face the inevitable conclusion of our time together.

"Hey, I told you I was a problem solver. It's what I do, it's what I'm good at. You needed something fixed so I fixed it, no matter the cost…that's how it works." He cocked an eyebrow and tilted his chin defiantly. "I think the words you're looking for are 'thank you'."

Angrily and desperately, I closed the space between us. I grabbed the front of his shirt and used my hold on the fabric to pull myself to the tips of my toes. I slammed my mouth on his and immediately tasted snow and man. His lips were chilly and his beard was damp from being outside, but his tongue was warm as it tangled with mine and his breath was hot as I stole it from him. He immediately took over the kiss, owning it, controlling it, feeding it with the scrape of his teeth and the twist of his tongue. His icy hands grasped each side of my face and held me to him as I wrapped my fingers around his wrist. His pulse hammered furiously against my fingertips, each beat another second slipping away, marching us toward our separate fates. I'd wasted a lot of time with the people in my life that I cared about; I refused to do that with this one. I only got him for a few heartbeats; I was going to make them matter.

When I pulled back, we both had heavy-lidded eyes and whisper breaths. I leaned forward so I could rest my forehead on his fuzzy chin, and rubbed it against the springy facial hair that lived there. I found the gentle scrape of it comforting and arousing. I wanted to feel it across the rest of my skin.

"I'm going to be gone in the morning, Ben. This is not a problem you have to fix. This is an experience you need to have before the opportunity passes. If your purpose was to save me then consider it mission accomplished." I pulled back so I could look up at him, seduction and salvation clear between every blink and in every breath. "Let me be the reward for a job well done. Let me show you that you are worth a second chance, that everyone can be saved, before our time runs out." I let go of his wrist and reached for the scar on his neck. I traced my fingers over the mark and brushed my thumb along his Adam's apple as he swallowed hard. "There's a reason that we were thrown together, Ben. We were supposed to be here. We were supposed to save each other." I pressed into him as hard as I could and moved my mouth to that ravaged side of his throat. "This is not a mistake; it's a moment we will have forever."

"You honestly think sex is going to fix everything that's wrong with us, Pop-Tart? Because I gotta tell ya, in my experience sex is where a lot of those problems I ended up having to fix in my old life started." He was on the edge; all I needed to do was push him over.

"No, I don't think sex will fix us, but I think the two of us together will give us something to hold onto when the days are dark and remind us that there is a reason to keep going. It will be a memory that makes sense when nothing else does. I want that so bad I can taste it." I smiled at him and reached up to push his coat off his wide shoulders. It hit the floor with a plop as I tugged at the Henley that was underneath and ordered him to unbuckle his belt. Being one handed sucked; it made getting to all the things I wanted to play with more difficult than it should be. I was impatient and anxious, racing against his resistance. "For the rest of your life, no matter what goes wrong or how bad things get, we'll have this single moment where we got everything right. Don't you need that? Because I know I do."

He grunted when his belt was finally free and I managed to get his zipper down. He was all kinds of hard covered in cotton and eagerly waiting to fall into my hands. I gave the impressive bulge a pat and used the pad of my thumb to trace the rigid line up where the tip was trapped under the stretchy band of his underwear. I stroked my fingers over the flared point and had to bite back a victory cheer when he leaned back against the door behind him with a thud as he pushed his clothing out of my way. His shirt landed on top of my bag and his jeans and briefs ended up around his knees as I leaned in closer to him, my hand working up and down the velvety, firm shaft.

I kissed his scar again and he surrendered on a sigh as he told me, "Save me or sacrifice me, I don't care which one it ends up being as long as I get my cock in your mouth and I get the chance to watch you come when I'm buried as deep as I can get inside of you." He pulled me up onto my toes once again and touched his lips to mine. I closed my hand around his cock reflexively and felt the vibration of his groan all the way into my core. It made my body throb and my nipples tighten instantly. When he released me, he did it with a smirk and a challenge in his eyes. "This has to be our moment, Echo, because it's so not perfect, but that doesn't matter because you kind of are. Show me what you got, Pop-Tart."

Challenge accepted.

I felt like I'd been waiting to show someone what I was really all about since the moment I made the decision to get clean and take my life back.

I kissed the hollow of his throat and slipped my thumb over the now damp slit on the crown of his cock. His hips involuntarily kicked toward me and his hands curled into fists at his sides. I nibbled on his collarbone and continued to work my fist up and down, feeling his body throb and heat in reaction. His already rigid abs tightened even more and his thick thighs clenched enticingly as I continued to work him with my hand and tease him with my mouth. He muttered my name and it had never sounded so much like a dirty word.

I flicked my tongue over the flat of his nipple and rubbed the tip of my nose against the brush of his chest hair as I moved over to repeat the action on the other side. He grunted and lifted his hands to rest them on my shoulders, but thought better of it when they automatically stiffened to protect the injured one. Instead, his fingers skimmed lightly through my hair and twined in the curls, holding on carefully as I methodically lowered myself to my knees in front of him, stopping to trace his taut tummy along the way.

I glanced up at him from under my lashes and felt my body clench at the sight of his locked jaw, hooded eyes, and flushed face. His broad chest was rising and falling like he was struggling to breathe and the veins in his biceps were lifted as he struggled to keep himself in control so he didn't force me or move me in a way that was going to jar my shoulder. He was a man used to taking what he wanted but in our moment, he was going to let me give it to him instead.

I followed the bold line of the vein that ran along the underside of his cock with my tongue and stopped to circle the head over and over again. I licked him like he was a lollipop and chased the moisture that trickled out of the tip until he moaned, his fingers twitching in silent demand against my scalp. I got the impression he wanted to pull, to tug, to guide me but he was forcing himself to stay in check because of my lingering injuries. "Put your lips around it, Echo."

I followed his order and immediately sucked so hard that my cheeks hollowed out. He was way too big to take all the way in, so I kept my hand circled around the base of his erection, turning and twisting in time to the gentle suction of my mouth. I liked the weight of him on my tongue, liked the way he took up all the space there was. It made me wet and had me squirming in front of him. Once again, I was irritated I couldn't use my left hand for much of anything. If it had been working the way it was supposed to, I would slip it under the baggy waistband of my borrowed pants and work on soothing the ache that was building between my thighs. I squeezed them together and moaned around the steely flesh in my mouth.

I took more of his length, pulling that pulsing flesh back as far as I could. I licked and sucked, swirled and twisted until he was panting loud enough that it blocked out the rush of my own arousal between my ears. His big body arched and bent before me. His hands left my hair, one going to cup my cheek, the other covering mine on the lower part of his erection. He tightened his fingers over mine, applying far more pressure than I would have dared for the first time. He squeezed and tugged as I swallowed and forced myself to breathe when he exploded across my tongue in a warm, wild rush. It was a little messy and a lot chaotic when he let his head fall back against the door while he stroked his thumb over the crest of my cheek. He was right; it wasn't exactly flawless—we were both too hurried and frantic trying to get as much of each other as we could. But he was as close to my perfect match as I'd ever found, so it was a moment that would stretch into infinity every time I thought about him and how special this time with someone that was made for me was.

I leaned back on my haunches and gazed up at him. His eyes had an edge that was sharp enough to slice right through my heart as he reached down and offered me a hand so he could help me to my feet.

We stared at each other silently for a long minute as he struggled to regulate his breathing and waited for his watery knees to hold him upright. Once he had his composure back, he reached for me, pulling me to his chest so that my head was tucked under his chin, his wet and slippery dick pressed against my middle, which made my blood heat and my heart trip over itself. I wanted it. I wanted him.

"All right, Pop-Tart, we have one day. Let's make enough memories to last us a lifetime." He kissed my temple and took my hand so he could guide me to the bed.

"Sounds good to me." In fact, I was pretty confident it was the only smart decision I'd made since saying goodbye to my sister.

I would never forget a single second of what being saved and being a savior felt like.

Chapter 8

Ben

For the first time since I'd started having sex way back in my early teens, I was *going* to bed with a woman. For once, I wasn't taking her there with ulterior motives. I wasn't tricking her, luring her, conning her, manipulating her, deceiving her, or employing any of the other underhanded ways I utilized in order to get my way and to get what I wanted.

In fact, she was leading the way. Her hand was wrapped around mine, long hair tangled down her naked back and playing peek-a-boo with the delicious dimples that rested right above the swell of her ass. When she looked at me over her shoulder, there was no hesitation in her brilliant blue gaze, only warm anticipation and swirling promises that I hoped she wouldn't regret keeping. I'd followed the wrong people in my life for a long time because they swore they could give me everything I wanted. Following her to the messy but inviting bed, I realized the bad people I'd trailed after when I was younger never had the ability to give me what I really wanted, what I had been searching for all along. I wanted to be accepted. I wanted to be forgiven for the mistakes I'd made. I wanted to be appreciated, faults and all, and I didn't want to take that respect through force and intimidation. I wanted to earn it. I wanted it to be mine free and clear.

I wanted someone to think I was worthy based on the fact that against all odds, against my own innate selfishness and overblown ego, I'd managed to do something right. I wanted someone to see I could put their needs above my own because even though I was a bad man, from an even worse place, I could recognize good when it landed in my lap.

Fortunately, what Echo was actually asking for was a whole lot easier and a whole lot more fun for me to give her. She wanted my hands all over that flawless skin. She wanted my mouth on her breasts. She wanted the scrape of my beard and the press of my much bigger, harder body into her smaller, softer one. More than all of that, she wanted my cock planted deep inside of her, filling her up, taking what she offered and giving back everything I had so she wouldn't be able to forget me tomorrow, or the day after that, or the one after that. She didn't want to feel empty anymore and I couldn't wait to be the one that took up all that space, made it my own, claimed it as mine, for however long our moment lasted.

She hit the edge of the bed and turned around so she could sit in front of me, my rock-hard dick right at her eye level. I reached out my hands so I could push the dark waves of her hair behind her shoulders and used my thumbs to trace the delicate line of her jaw. I tilted her head back so that she was looking up at me and bent down so I could kiss the tip of her nose as she put her hand on the side of my hip. Her thumb dug into the sharp V of muscle that cut along the side of my abs and I couldn't hold back a smirk when she sighed in appreciation. In my old line of work, it was a bad idea to have any kind of weakness, so I always made sure I could hold my own with the brawlers that ran the streets. Being in decent shape was an asset in prison as well. The phrase "too pretty to be locked up" had merit, so it was good I could take care of myself when I needed to, but that was all practical, necessary even. I used the way I looked as a weapon and as a tool, but knowing Echo liked what she saw when she looked at me was the first time I'd ever been thankful for genetics and endless hours spent in the gym. I needed to get back to it and stop using my circumstances as an excuse for letting my entire life slip away.

I brushed my nose over the arch of her cheek and used the tip of my tongue to trace the outside of her earlobe as she leaned backward, her shoulders hitting the mattress while I hovered over her. I ran my fingers down the elegant column of her neck and stopped to stroke the place where I could feel her pulse racing. There wasn't an ounce of fear coming off of her, which was good because I had enough for both of us.

I was worried I was going to hurt her, physically and emotionally. I was worried that she was going to hurt me…and I had no idea how I would handle that. My guess was not very well. She wanted this moment to count, wanted to make memories that would last a lifetime and I was terrified I was going to disappoint her and those memories would end up as nightmares she couldn't escape from.

"I need to get the condoms that are in the first aid kit and we both need to pray to every single higher power that might exist that they're not expired." I dropped a hard kiss on her parted lips and took a step back. "We're also going to have to get creative with that busted wing of yours. I've been living like a monk in this monastery and was locked up for longer than I want to think about before that. I want to be gentle and considerate with you, but when you let a wild animal out of a cage, it can be impossible to control."

She tossed her head back and laughed at my graphic analogy and again I was amazed at how effortless everything with her seemed to be. She should be running away but instead, she reached out and traced the underside of my cock with her finger. It jerked at the gentle touch and my stomach tightened.

Mirth and amusement battled with arousal and excitement in her eyes. "I'm not worried about getting bit. In fact, I'm kind of looking forward to it." She curled her fingers around my erection and gave the shaft a squeeze that had my eyes rolling back into my head. "If you're as good with this as you are with your mouth, I won't be able to feel any pain I might be in over the pleasure. I can't wait for that kind of painkiller." She licked her lower lip and I immediately slicked my tongue over the wet trail she left, savoring her flavor and letting my teeth sink into the plump curve, taking my first bite.

Her fingers tightened around my cock, making me put my hand around her wrist and pulling it off before I got so lost in what she was doing to me and what she was begging me with her eyes to do to her that I forgot protection. I vowed to take care of her, and making sure she made it off this mountain with memories and nothing more than that was part of it. I kissed her again and dashed to the bathroom so I could scavenge through the white box that I'd used to patch her up that first night. Someone had told me the condoms were actually to keep ammunition and firearms dry in an emergency. I didn't give a shit why they were in the cabin; I was simply grateful that they were. Because all the stars seemed to have aligned the night she tumbled into my arms, the condoms were good and there were plenty of them to get us through the night.

I walked back to where she was still perched on the edge of the bed and tossed the sleeve on top of the quilt. Now that I knew we were good to go, there was no stopping the rush of blood and shot of adrenaline-laced anticipation that worked through me. She looked better than a way out of jail. She felt better than a promise of a future outside of the Point. She smelled better than wealth and extravagance. She sounded better than all the lies I'd convinced myself were the truth.

I kissed her and took her back down to the mattress. I ran my hand over her collarbone and across the swell of her breast. I covered the sweet skin with my palm and rubbed steady circles over the crest until her nipple beaded and poked anxiously into my touch. Once both peaks were pebbled and hard, stained ruby red with arousal, I moved my mouth to one pointed tip and sucked it into the warm cavern of my mouth. I trapped the opposite side between my fingers and tugged. The motion brought her shoulders up off the bed, which made her wince and had her good arm curling around my shoulders so she could hold herself still while I sucked on her and nibbled on her delectable flesh.

I trailed my mouth along the valley between her breasts, stopping to leave biting, stinging kisses along the way and admiring the way my beard left her porcelain skin pink. There would be no missing where I had been. There would be a map of pleasure for her to follow when we were no longer in the same life. She wouldn't be able to wash me away or wipe me off, and that made my dick throb and my hands harder than they should have been as I held her to my mouth and tortured her other nipple with teeth and tongue.

She whimpered below me, legs falling open and her hand sliding its way along my back and across my hip until she could reach the erection between my legs that was pointing right at her. I jolted as she circled the tip with her thumb, bending the rigid shaft toward her wet center. She arched more fully into me, pushing more of her full breast into my mouth, moaning my name when I used my teeth with more force than I intended to. She put a heel on the edge of the bed and let her leg fall to the side so she was wide open and exposed. I grunted in response, my breath locking in suddenly seized lungs as she maneuvered the crown of my dick against her slick folds and started to lift her hips and grind against the hardness.

"Fuck me."

I couldn't stop myself from moving, from rocking into that heat and wetness. I could feel the bud of her clit rubbing eagerly along the underside of my cock and it was enough to make me forget my own name. "You don't fuck fair." I was trying to take my time, to make every second we had count and she was pushing me toward the point of no return.

She used the moisture my dick was spreading around to glide her hand over the topside of my dick as she continued to pull me through her folds and rock her clit against me. She was panting underneath me and her eyes were at half-mast as a small smile played around her mouth.

"I see that newfound integrity of yours trying to make an appearance. I'm beating it to the punch." She lifted her leg and wrapped it around my waist as just the tip, the leaking, aching tip hit her soft spot and sank inside. It was barely anything, but both of us groaned at the contact and went still as the impact of how it felt to be together, the power of being with someone that understood exactly what they were getting from the other with no unrealistic expectation hit us.

She was right. This was right.

This was the only moment in my entire life where I knew I was exactly where I was supposed to be, doing precisely what I was supposed to be doing.

I let her fall back to the mattress with a little thud and pushed deeper into her. I couldn't bottom out, thrust into her with the wild abandon that I wanted to without a condom on, but I wanted to know how she would feel. I didn't want to be able to wash her off or wipe her away either. The press of my hips into hers made her body move on the bed and we both went still as she sucked in a sharp breath and let out a cry of pain. It wasn't the good kind.

She blinked wide eyes up at me and wiggled where she was impaled on my greedy cock. Her eyebrows lifted and she moved her good hand to the center of my chest, where she raked her fingers through my chest hair. "That's not going to work."

I snorted out a laugh and pulled out of her body. My dick was instantly furious with me and I smiled at her as a frown pulled at her pretty features at the loss of our connection.

No one ever missed me when I was gone, but she couldn't even stand the scant few inches that separated us. It made me feel more powerful and more important than anything in my life ever had.

"I told you, I solve problems and I always figure out a solution." I lowered my head so I could kiss the tip of each of her breasts, then crawled up and over her, making sure to keep clear of her long hair as I went. I didn't want to pull on it in case the cut on her scalp was still tender. I put my back to the wall and stretched my legs out in front of me, crooking a finger at her. "Come over here and bring the condoms with you."

She twisted around, grabbed the packet like I asked, and then inched on her knees so she was kneeling next to me. I put my hands on her hips as she straddled me and then took the rubbers from her so I could cover myself since there was no way she could do it with one hand. She curled her arm around my neck and was nuzzling her nose into the side of my throat, her damp tongue darting out to taste my skin. I shivered all over when she traced my scar from where it started behind my ear to where it ended at the hollow of my throat with a long, wet swipe. I wanted to tell her to stop. I was scared she could taste how dirty and vile all the things that had led up to me earning that mark were. It was my fate carved into my skin and I didn't want her corrupted by what was. I wanted her turned on and dreaming of what could be.

Once I was sheathed in latex, I wrapped my hands in her hair and pulled her far enough away from my chest that I could look her in the eyes. The blue of her gaze blazed like a torch and the flush in her face made her look like the fairytale princess I'd accused her of being.

"We need to keep your shoulder still and braced the best we can. You aren't ready to ride yet, Pop-Tart. And as much as I love the idea of getting to watch those unbelievable tits bouncing while you fuck me, the idea of how uncomfortable that will be for you kills my hard-on. I think what we need to do is flip the script." I lifted my chin and circled a finger in the air in front of her wide eyes. "Turn around and face away from me." She lifted a questioning eyebrow but did as I said. I groaned at the vision of her perfectly rounded ass nestled against my groin and couldn't resist taking a minute to trace the adorable little divots she had at the base of her spine. "Sit on my cock, Echo. Take me all the way in and once I'm as deep as I can go, lean back against my chest so I can hold your upper body still while we tear each other apart."

She put her working hand on my thigh and crossed the other one protectively over her chest. She looked at me over her shoulder, watching as I stopped breathing, stopped thinking, stopped functioning when she started to take me slowly into her welcoming body. She was molten hot and silky smooth. She was tight and fitted around me like she was custom made to take my cock. She pulsed in time to my heartbeat and whispered my name like it was the only word she remembered how to say.

Our bodies instinctively moved together, straining and aching to get closer. The steady stretch of her body as she made room for me had me lifting one of my hands back up to her breast so I could roll her nipple between my fingers. I growled dirty words in her ear the wetter and looser she got around me. The dual stimulation had the grip and pull of her inner walls lightening and with a sudden shift I was seated all the way inside of her and seeing stars. Even with the barrier of the condom, I could feel every pulse, every throb, and every tremor of her pussy. She felt electric and alive. She felt unforgettable.

Once she had every hard, solid inch of me inside of her, she leaned back like a good girl, her head on my shoulder as I locked one of my arms around where she was holding herself like a vise. Her hair was everywhere and her shoulders were shaking. I kissed the shell of her ear and took her good hand in mine as I started to move underneath her. It took some finesse and some finagling to figure out how I could thrust up into her while keeping her braced against my chest. It was a little bit sloppy and a whole lot of effort, but the way her body clamped down on mine, the way she went liquid and started to mewl her pleasure, meant I found a way to rock up into her over and over again, hitting her sweet spot every time my hips kicked upwards.

I dragged her trapped hand over her chest and across her abraded and swollen nipples. I tugged the compliant digits over her belly and down below her waist. Once I hit wet, I put our combined hands over her slippery center and pressed down on her exposed clit. I could feel the sharp edge of her nails on my cock as I continued to power my way inside of her.

I used my control of her hand to guide her into touching herself. I ordered her to stroke her clit, to circle it and fondle it until she couldn't take it anymore. She did everything I told her to do, including making sure she rubbed her knuckles along my shaft every time I hammered my way home. She was so ridiculously perfect. So outrageously ideal I couldn't take much more.

I lifted my free hand that wasn't holding her prisoner to her neck and carefully wrapped my fingers around her throat. In her ear, I whispered that I wanted to feel the way I made her heart beat. I told her I wanted to catch every moan, every scream, every whisper I ripped out of her body. They were all mine and I was keeping them so I could relive them once it was just me and the mountain once again. I tightened my hold, squeezing as her body quickened around mine with each new declaration.

"I'm so close." She whimpered the warning and tilted her head to the side so I could catch the corner of her gaze.

I chuckled and used my teeth on her ear as I threw my hips up over and over again. "I will follow you wherever you lead, Echo." Because of her, I finally knew where I was going.

My grasp on her neck tightened a little more, making her fingers move furiously between her legs. My pulse pounded, my cock stretched and pulsed. Her heart thundered erratically and her breathing went shallow and choppy. I felt pleasure unfurl low in my spine as my balls drew up tight and close to my body. She pressed her shoulders back into my chest like she was trying to force her way inside my skin. A second later, I felt her break. A warm rush of liquid covered my cock and her quivering thighs tensed and shifted where they were braced on the outside of mine.

That flood of pleasure and the fluttering of her body as she moved around me was all it took for me to find my own release. I growled her name into her uncontrollable mane of hair, moved my hand to her jaw so I could lift her face up to mine so that we were cheek to cheek, and unleashed everything I had built up inside into her greedy center. She milked me dry. She took everything I had and then caressed me slow and sweet until I came back down from the stratosphere she had launched me into.

I might have turned over a new leaf the day I found her, but right here, right now, I knew I was a new man because of her. It only took a look and I wanted to be someone different, someone that did, in fact, deserve a second chance and a shot at some kind of redemption.

I kissed her cheek and smoothed a hand over her torso. She didn't seem like she was in any hurry to move and I was happy with her exactly where she was.

"Everything feel okay? We didn't jam the shoulder back up, did we?" She'd done a lot of moaning and groaning but none of it sounded like it came from pain.

She was quiet for a long time. So long that I was starting to worry and was going to pull out of her and roll her over so I could demand to know what was wrong when she finally cocked her good arm up around my head and muttered so low that I almost didn't hear her, "Everything feels more than okay. It feels better than it has since…well, forever. I was savoring the moment."

This girl.

She was going to end me. Others had tried…but only this broken woman could do it.

My life had been spent making sure people couldn't wait to get rid of me. I'd made it a point to make sure they didn't want to be in my company for any longer than they had to and here she was savoring me…savoring our moment.

How was I supposed to let her go when she was the only one that wanted me?

Chapter 9

Echo

All the things in life that were bad for you, that you were supposed to stay away from, and protect yourself from sure felt really good and were a lot more fun than the things that were healthy and good for you.

Drugs.

Junk food.

Endless hours of television.

A day spent doing nothing but having mind-blowing sex with a dangerous man I would never see again.

All of those things were addicting, but I knew instinctively the one I was going to have the hardest time quitting was the last one. Getting clean sucked. It left me wrung out and hollow on the inside. It left me feeling itchy and restless, always pushing back the urge to fade away and forget. It left me weak and lost. I'd always had a crutch to fall back on, an easy excuse to hand over whenever I messed up or made a mistake that hurt someone, a justification for why I was always hurting myself. It took a long time and lots of help to find my footing after I kicked the habit and there was a cold knot of fear in my chest that it was going to take a shitload more than that to get over my newest addiction.

We spent the rest of the day and all of the evening after Ben went and found my stuff wrapped up in each other. I learned that sex, when you had to get creative because of limitations, could be the most fun two people had together. I learned he was arrogant and bossy in bed just like he was out of it, and I was surprised to find that I didn't mind taking orders and doing what I was told if it meant I got him inside of me faster. I'd taken control of my life in an iron fist when I decided to get clean. I held onto my sobriety with a grip that was unbreakable and, frankly, exhausting. It was refreshing to let my hold loosen and let someone else be in charge of making sure things happened the way they were supposed to, that nothing went off course.

I also learned that he could be gentle, but I preferred it when he was rough. Ben was a big man, with hard hands and sharp eyes. When he was soft and sweet, it melted something inside of me, something I didn't know was frozen until he touched it. When he was impatient and hungry, when he was demanding and forceful, I didn't melt…I burned. I lit up from the inside and I was pretty sure that made me glow on the outside. I'd never been the type of woman that glowed. I never felt bright enough, shiny enough, happy enough to glow. But Ben and his ragged voice and dirty words rasped harshly in my ear got me there and I didn't want to ever go back to being dull and lifeless.

I also learned I could deep throat like a champ when I was inspired and that when a man with a beard and a talented tongue told you to sit on his face, you should never, ever refuse him. He made me see stars multiple times; even when I thought I was too tired, too sore, too spent for anything, he always managed to wring one last response out of me. It was like he was making up for all the forgettable sex I'd had in the past with men who would never matter. He was filling every single second of the moment we were in with experiences that would be impossible to top or outdo. No man was ever going to compare; he made sure of it and that twisted my heart into knots because when the sun came up in the morning and the doctor with the sexy voice showed up to take me back to town with him, our moment would be gone and I would spend the rest of my life searching for something that came slightly close to these stolen hours with a man I wasn't supposed to know and couldn't have.

After a shower that was more just the two of us rubbing our wet, slippery selves against one another, Ben told me he was going to take that beater of a pickup truck that suited him about as well as the flannel, up to the road to make sure the doc could get in. If he hadn't said the words quietly and thoughtfully, I would have assumed he was anxious to get rid of me. But he had been watching me all morning long and I could practically see the wheels turning in his handsome head. He couldn't go and I couldn't stay, which was a problem…and he was good at figuring out solutions to problems. I let him go without a fuss, figuring he needed the time to get his thoughts and feelings in order before our fantasy was shattered by the harsh light of reality.

I believed if he really wanted to, he would figure out a way to get himself off of this mountain. But I was also used to disappointment and things not working out the way I wanted them to, so Ben was going to have to forgive me for stacking the deck in my favor. I crept over to the closet and dug around until my fingers landed on that ridiculously expensive watch he had stashed there. He might not want to claim me once I was out of his hair and out of sight, but there was no way he was going to let a watch that cost as much as single family home go without some effort to get it back.

When he came back, it was the sound of two engines, not one, rumbling outside the small cabin. I peeked out the window as an attractive man, several years older than both me and Ben, was climbing out of a pickup truck. He was tall, broad shouldered with dark hair, and what looked like an easy smile. He was far better looking than most of the doctors I'd ever been under the care of. Much more rugged and capable looking. I doubted he played golf on the weekends. He said something to Ben which made him scowl and turned toward the house without waiting for Ben to respond.

The doctor's footsteps were heavy on the stairs leading up to the door and his knock was brisk as he pounded on the door mere seconds before walking in. "Echo, I'm Thomas MacKenzie. Let's get you checked out and off this mountain before another storm moves in. I'm sure you're ready to get back home."

I wasn't ready, but I'd learned long ago that running away from the things I didn't want to face didn't lead to anywhere good. I reached out and shook the hand he offered, taking a moment to really look at him. "Thank you for going out of your way to come and get me. I'm sure you're busy, being the only doctor around for miles."

I wondered if he could be the one. Was he the man my sister was so sure was the one meant for her? He was without question an extremely good looking man, and his smile was contagious, but there was something in his manner, an abruptness and dismissiveness that I couldn't see Xanthe gravitating to. Faced with the potent MacKenzie charisma, it was easier for me to see why she had fallen and fallen hard.

"No problem. We look after everyone who wanders into our neck of the woods. A lot of folks come up here not understanding how dangerous it can be. You're far from the first stranded tourist I've had to rescue." He looked over his shoulder as the door opened and Ben came into the room. His eyes landed on me and then skimmed over the man in front of me as his beard twitched when he frowned. "You're lucky you crashed so close to Ben's cabin. A little farther up the road and no one would have heard a thing. You would have been stuck out in the snow until the road crews came through with the plows. All in all, you were very lucky."

I lifted an eyebrow in Ben's direction. "I am lucky."

The doctor shifted his gaze between the two of us and cleared his throat when the tension in the room became palpable. "Have a seat and let me look you over. Not much we can do for your shoulder other than put your arm in a sling. The upside of that is other travelers will feel bad for you because you only have one hand and offer to help you out." He grinned at me and I couldn't resist grinning back.

I took a seat on the edge of the bed and let him poke and prod at me. I winced when he moved my hair to look at the wound on my head, tugging harder than Ben had been over the last few days. It was starting to heal but still sore. I also cringed when he tugged on my injured arm but none of it made my vision blur or my nerves fire off with unbearable pain. He listened to my heart with a stethoscope he pulled out of his coat pocket and shined a light in my eyes which made me sneeze. It was probably the quickest exam I'd ever been given but considering my injuries were a couple of days old and Ben had done his best to fix me up, there wasn't much for Thomas to do.

He ordered me to take a couple of Tylenol for my shoulder, cast one last look between me and Ben, and told me he would be waiting in the truck when I was ready to head down the mountain.

Once Ben and I were alone, the air in the room around us felt like it got heavy. Every molecule was filled with all the things we wanted to say but couldn't. We'd been racing toward this moment from the moment he saved me. I didn't want to say goodbye but I couldn't say until we meet again because that would give me hope when I didn't really have any.

I walked over to where he was leaning against the counter, hands braced in front of the sink. I put a hand on the center of his chest and looked up at him. I forced a lopsided grin and tapped my fingers on the front of his shirt to the erratic beat of his heart.

"You have a problem, Ben." I leaned into him so I could kiss that line on his throat that had nearly stolen his life away. "You met a girl in the wrong place, at the wrong time, but there is no arguing she is the right girl for you." I pulled back and sighed as his hands lifted so he could pull my entire body into his. It was a hug that warmed me up from the top of my head to the tip of my toes. "She's counting on you to figure out a way to make it work because she is very good at causing problems and you are very good at solving them."

I felt him brush a kiss across the crown of my head and his fingertips dug painfully into the curve of my hips.

I wrapped an arm around his neck and pulled his head toward mine. It was a kiss that changed me. It was a kiss that shaped me into a woman that knew I could make the hard choices for the right reasons. It was a kiss that told me I could walk away from temptation and enticement when I had to. It was a kiss that had every right thing I'd ever done in it. It was a kiss that told me Ben was saved and let me know I was the one that had saved him.

His lips were hard against mine, punishing. He didn't like this any better than I did and it was killing him that there was nothing either of us could do about it. I wasn't supposed to be here…and neither was he. He needed to find a way to get his life back, now that he had one worth living and now that he was a man trying to be worthy of living it.

When I pulled back, we were both breathing hard and his jaw was locking in a line so tight I was worried his back teeth might crack. I rubbed my thumb along his now damp lower lip.

"This girl…she's going to miss you, Ben." I took a step back and he let his hands fall. He exhaled long and low, his eyes sharp enough to slice through all my bravado and bluster. "She's also a thief. I took something you're going to want back, so even if you can't figure out a way to come for me, you're going to want to figure out a way to come for what I stole."

His lips twitched in response but he didn't make a move toward me until I bent to pick up my battered bag. I didn't even have the handles in my hand when he was there hefting it up and putting a hand on my lower back so he could guide me out the door and down to the waiting truck. The engine was running and the doctor was behind the wheel tapping his fingers and looking at his cell phone. Ben walked me to the passenger door, stopping to pull it open so he could deposit the bag on the floorboard. I felt his fingers at the back of my neck, under my hair, and his lips touch the top of my ear.

"You were never a problem, Echo. You have been nothing but a pleasure from the get go." He squeezed my neck and stepped back as I turned around to look at him. "Take care of yourself, Pop-Tart."

I dipped my chin down and blinked away the sudden wash of tears that filled my eyes. "You too, and, Ben…" His eyes burned into mine, searing the last few days deep into my soul. "Keep the beard. That's the one part of this life that does suit you."

He helped me up into the truck and closed the door with a soft *click*. I gave him a little wave and got a very masculine chin lift in response. I was trying to hold it together—after all, I'd lost so much more than a man I'd only had for a moment—but I couldn't stop a couple of stray teardrops from rolling over my eyelashes and running down my too-hot cheeks. I swiped at the telltale sign of weakness with the back of my hand and let out a shuddering sigh.

I could feel the man next to me looking at me out of the corner of his very blue eyes. I didn't have the emotional reserves left to deal with his sympathy or his suspicion. Fortunately, he seemed pretty attuned to the fact that I was on the edge and ready to slip over, so all he offered up was a quiet, "Been an intense few days for you, hasn't it?"

I sighed again and leaned over so I could rest my forehead on the cool glass of the window. "You have no idea."

Everything was a white blur as he navigated away from the cabin on a road that wasn't much of a road at all. Ben was literally hidden away from everything and everyone. I never would have found him if I hadn't gone careening down that mountain on the worst night of my life.

"Everything will settle down and seem less catastrophic once you're back in familiar territory." His voice was low and soothing. He might have been in a hurry but his impeccable bedside manner never wavered.

"Maybe, but I tend to live in chaos. This was actually a nice break from the insanity I surround myself in." Ben had been the shelter to my always raging storm. "But every fairy tale ends. Snow White has to wake up and face the music eventually."

He had no idea what I was talking about, which was fine by me. I wasn't sure I could put into words the enormity of what I felt toward Ben and my time with him. Turning my head slightly, I asked, "Did any of your brothers ever mention a girl that worked at the airport in Denver paying a lot of unwanted attention to them, by any chance?"

He gave me a questioning look and lifted a shoulder in a careless shrug. "No, but all of us usually have a layover in Denver when we travel out of state; why?"

It was my turn to shrug. "My sister worked in the airport. She mentioned a MacKenzie that left quite an impression on her. That's why I'm in Surrender. She talked about it all the time. She wanted to come here but she passed away recently." I turned back to look at the trees passing by alarmingly close to the windows. "I came here for her, because she would never get the chance."

"I thought you were meeting friends? Isn't that what Ben told Cooper?" Now there was suspicion in his tone, making it sharp and hard.

"Ben lied. He told me I was chasing ghosts and he was right. He didn't want the sheriff to think I was some crazy woman that had purposely driven off the side of the road because of her grief." It was stretching the truth just a little. I couldn't very well tell Thomas that Ben didn't want me ruffling any MacKenzie feathers unjustly.

"Ben likes to play fast and loose with the truth, doesn't he?" My executive lumberjack was always going to be an outsider while he was stuck up here living a life that wasn't his.

"I think that's a survival mechanism. Sometimes, you have to tell yourself so many lies that you can't even recognize what the truth is anymore." Right now, I was lying to myself and not doing a very good job of it.

Over and over again, I silently chanted, *everything is going to be fine*, but I was having a hard time believing it. Nothing felt fine. It felt awful and empty.

"I have a younger brother, Shane. He's actually the youngest of all of us and he's always been kind of a wildcard. He's restless, has a knack for trouble, and lives for a good time. His life went a little sideways recently, but before that upset, I wouldn't be surprised if he was the one that caught your sister's eye. He's a flirt and a charmer without trying to be either. Women tend to fall at his feet and he's gotten used to maneuvering around them as delicately as he can." There was pride and hard-won understanding throughout his tone.

I thought having an idea, having a tangible person to hang all my grief and sorrow on would help. It didn't. Ben was right. All I felt was understanding and the familiar thrum of pain that echoed inside of me when I thought about Xanthe. I was an older sibling with a wayward younger sibling, so I understood every ounce of emotion the doctor had in his voice. We loved, even when those we cared for made it really hard to do so. "I'm glad I got the chance to see the place she dreamed of. It was worth the trip."

It was so worth it.

Chapter 10

Benny

I spent the first week after Echo left moping and feeling sorry for myself.

I spent the second week plotting and planning. I made myself dizzy trying to figure out a way off the mountain, but every direction I turned led to me dragging her into a mess she didn't need to be in. The feds weren't going to let me go, not when they thought they could still use me, and if I went off the reservation, they would stop at nothing until they found me. It would put Echo directly in the center of law enforcement crosshairs if I took off and they found her with me. It wasn't like I could ask them for any favors either. They'd dropped me in the middle of nowhere Montana for a reason. I hadn't earned my way out of prison based on good behavior. No one in their right mind was going to go out of their way to make my life a little easier and a whole lot more pleasurable by moving me to an actual city with a population of more than a couple thousand. To them, keeping me breathing and putting a roof over my head was good enough. This was all the consideration I deserved after the kind of life I'd lived and the things I had done.

The third week I convinced myself it was all the intensity of the situation and emotions running high because of how long I'd been without a woman, or without any kind of company really. I told myself it was a fluke, that I couldn't really be that twisted up and upside down over a girl I'd only known a couple of days. I blamed cabin fever and ordered myself to finally settle in and start appreciating the second chance I'd been given. I polished myself up, got back into the habit of taking care of myself, working out around the cabin and running when the weather cooperated. I slapped on the smile that used to get me whatever I wanted back home, and went on the prowl. These ski bunnies didn't stand a chance. I was going to gorge myself, stuff myself full of sex and satisfaction so there was no room for the uneasy ache that now seemed to live around my heart.

I quickly came to the conclusion that I was a fantastic liar, but there was no way I was going to buy in to my own bullshit. After dismissing the tenth or eleventh girl who made it clear she would be up for some no-strings vacation sex, for reasons that were ridiculous and reaching, I realized there was no way I was going to get over what I was feeling for Echo by getting inside someone else. It was fucking depressing, so I spent another week moping and feeling out of control because I couldn't get a handle on how to make the situation any better. The only things in this life I'd ever been good at were figuring out a way to fix things, and making people do what I wanted them to do so they were part of the solution, not part of the problem. There was no force to be used here, no knees to break or threats to throw around. There was no manipulation to be had and no strings to pull to get my way. I was stuck, dead in the water and the shore I wanted to reach seemed ridiculously out of my grasp.

It was toward the end of week six and the emptiness and loneliness that surrounded me were now like old friends. I woke up with them, went to bed with them, and to change things up so I didn't get totally bored, I gave them a rest and had breakfast and dinner with helplessness and self-loathing. I wondered if Echo was feeling as despondent and untethered as I was. I hated myself for being the kind of man that deserved being dumped in the middle of nowhere with nothing to do but think about every single thing he'd done in his life that led him there. She was better off without me. She deserved someone that could help her heal. She deserved someone that wouldn't take anything more from her, considering all that she had already given.

I was in the shower, spending time with my fist and memories, when it felt like the air in the cabin changed. It was like an electrical current was suddenly charging the tiny interior space. Every breath I took and exhaled felt alive as I slowly stopped what I was doing and moved to put a towel around my waist. It had been a hot minute since I'd been back home but there were some things that I would never forget about growing up and climbing my way to the top of the food chain in the Point. One of those things was the way that every sense seemed to sharpen and heighten when danger was close by. I could feel the prick of it against my skin. I could see the way the unknown made my skin pebble and the hair on my arms raise up. I could hear my heartbeat, fast and furious, between my ears, and I could taste the tang of fear and anticipation on my tongue. And the smell, well, the smell of danger in the Point came in a lot of different varieties but this was one that I knew all too well. It was the scent of expensive cologne and high-end products. It was the same scent that had clung to me when I used to be the danger the Point needed protection from.

Pushing my hands through my wet hair, I exited the bathroom and wasn't surprised at all to see a dark-haired man leaning against my rickety kitchen counter while another man messed with the shotgun that was leaning against the wall. Both were dressed in impeccably tailored suits and had on shoes that cost a pretty penny and would more than likely be ruined by the time they got off my mountain. In another life, Nassir Gates had been the kind of badass I tried to emulate. My old boss didn't believe in looking the part of a man in charge, but Nassir always had. He dressed like he was the one running the show, long before he'd taken the reins. I'd always admired his style, even though he was the only person I'd ever encountered in all my years of making people beg and bleed that scared the ever living shit out of me.

Novak had been a crazed madman, hell-bent on carnage and corruption. He was more than willing to let the entire city burn, and all the people that called it home could go with it for all he cared. Nassir was the opposite. Wickedly smart and coolly conniving, he didn't make a single move without thinking it through to the end. He was just as vicious, just as brutal as Novak had been, but instead of tearing the city down and walking all over the inhabitants, he was building it up and giving them the choice to stay or go. If you stayed, you accepted that the Point was never going to be easy and the men in charge were never going to be law-abiding and above board. If you left, you did so knowing that the secrets of the Point stayed locked within the grit and the grime. You didn't take what happened in the Point outside of the crumbling city and if you did, Nassir had a reach that was long and impossible to duck.

"I always wanted to try fly fishing. I've heard it's very relaxing. They teach you how to do that out here, Benny?"

The words came from Chuck, Nassir's right-hand man. The large African-American man had also been part of Novak's crew when I was running the streets, but before things went to shit, he got in good with Nassir, obviously smart enough to see the writing on the wall. The tides were getting ready to turn, the people that had nothing to lose suddenly had their hearts tangled up in good women, and that made them far more dangerous than Novak had ever managed to be.

"I'm sure they would if I asked, but standing in the middle of a cold-ass river all day isn't my idea of fun. What are you doing here, Gates?" I didn't bother to ask how he'd found me. Witness protection was supposed to be foolproof, but there wasn't much Nassir didn't know and there wasn't a single branch of the government or law enforcement that he didn't have some kind of dirt on. Novak had been a thug and brute. Nassir was a goddamn criminal mastermind. No one was better at giving just enough rope for you to hang yourself with. He'd let you twist and kick in the wind and then offer to save you, but only if you agreed that you owed him a favor.

Nassir's arms were crossed across his chest and I noticed he had a new tattoo on the back of his hand. It looked like an ornate lock attached to a chain. The guy could give Cumberbatch and Hiddleston a run for their money when it came to being suave and sophisticated, but underneath that Italian suit was a man ripped from the very bowels of hell and he had the ink and scars to prove it.

Everyone from the Point wore their secrets and scars with pride.

"Maybe I just missed your smiling face." His voice had the barest hint of an accent I could never pin down the origins of. When he spoke, it was both lethal and lyrical. "Nice face fuzz, by the way. Very mountain man."

I grunted and put my hands on my hips. I wasn't worried that they were here to kill me. If Nassir wanted me dead, there would be no conversation, just a bullet right between the eyes. He wasn't a man who offered explanation or excuses.

"It helps cover up the fact that my head was almost removed from my body while I was in lockup. You have anything to do with that?" I ran my thumb along my scar and narrowed my eyes at him.

He shook his head and looked over at Chuck, who offered up a shrug. "It wasn't us. We would have made sure the job was done right, not some half-assed shit like that. But you don't have many friends left back home, so I can't say I'm surprised someone tried to take you out."

Suddenly, exhausted from thinking about how hard it had been to keep myself alive for thirty years, I narrowed my eyes at Nassir and copied his pose, with my arms crossed over my chest. Of course, it looked much more intimidating and badass in the suit than it did in the towel, but whatever. "Tell me what you want or get the fuck out. I'm not in the mood for games and if the feds find out you're here, they'll send my ass back to lockup or move me somewhere even more remote than this mountain." My stomach clenched at the thought of how much harder it would be to get to Echo if they did either of those things.

Nassir's dark eyebrows lifted and Chuck let out a low chuckle. Clearly, putting on pants before confronting two of the most dangerous men I had ever met would have been a good idea.

"I have a problem." Nassir lifted a hand and ran it over his mouth while looking at me. "There's a girl that went missing and we've been unable to find her. One of my people is heavily invested in locating her and I have no intention of letting him down. All my regular sources have failed, so I'm coming to you. Everyone knows there isn't a problem you can't solve, Benny."

I rocked back on my heels a little bit and blinked at him in surprise. Of all the things he might have said, that wasn't something I was prepared for. "You have your fingers in every single pot in the Point. How is it you've managed to come up empty handed and need a Hail Mary? That's not your style, Gates."

"The pots my fingers are in don't sit on stoves up on the Hill. The only information we have on the girl that's missing was that she was doing her best to help the mayor's stepdaughter disappear. The players have dirty hands in an entirely different way than I'm used to dealing with. They are covered in white gloves and go pinky up during high tea." The Hill was the opulent, expensive part of the city, the polar opposite of the Point. I, however, knew that there was just as much crime and exploitation happening behind those closed mansion doors as there was on the streets. "No one will talk and time is running out. Help me find the girl and I will get you off this mountain."

I tossed my head back and laughed up at the ceiling. "Right. You're going to get me out of my deal with the feds like it's no big deal. You're good, Gates, but not that good."

He grinned at me and I felt my blood run cold. I should have known better than to question a man who didn't flinch when the fires of hell burned all around him.

"I know a Marshal. He helped out when Novak went down and everyone was trying to take over his spot. The city was at war and the Marshal stepped in to try and keep the body count to a minimum. He's agreed to take over your case, after I blackmailed his boss into agreeing to let me pull you out of the program. You help find the girl and I'll let you go. You can relocate anywhere in the world you want to, but you still have to cooperate with the feds if they think you have information that might help them take down Novak's old suppliers and obviously, you'll owe me a favor if I should ever need your special brand of problem solving in the future."

I shook my head a little, my thoughts pinging and buzzing around my brain like angry bees. "You blackmailed a federal agent?"

He shrugged as if to say "I do it all the time". "He should be better about hiding the fact he likes to play the ponies and drown his sorrow in barely legal male prostitutes when he doesn't win. His wife is a Congresswoman and wouldn't take too kindly to that information going public. For some reason, the people with the most to lose are always the ones with the most to hide."

I cocked my head to the side and considered him thoughtfully for a long, silent moment. "Bax will finish the job that was started when I was locked up if I come back to the Point. He's not going to overlook the fact I broke his best friend's legs and snatched his girl up and handed her over to Novak. I stood there and did nothing while he cut her open, Gates. Bax isn't the kind to forgive and forget." And I couldn't blame him. I would want me dead too if the situation was reversed and I was the one watching a monster torture the woman I loved because of someone like me.

Nassir nodded and Chuck let out a grunt of agreement. "You're right. Bax would have you in a shallow grave in no time at all. But in order to do that he would have to know you were back on the streets. He's in Denver right now with Dovie. That teenager they are all so determined to get out of the city decided to go to college in Boulder. Bax and the entire crew took a week off to move her. You have exactly four days to get in, get me the info I need on the girl, and get out before all hell will break loose."

It was so tempting. He was offering me the solution to the problem I couldn't fix on my own, but I was leery of making any kind of deal with the devil. "What if I can't find her? What happens to me if I don't manage to hold up my end of the bargain?" I'd never failed before but there was a first time for everything.

Nassir pushed off the counter and lifted his chin up so that he was looking down his nose at me. I hated that it felt like he could see right through me. "If you want off this mountain badly enough, you won't fail. This is the only chance you've got, Ben. I would make it count if I were you. I'm offering you all the best parts of your old life back and don't bother telling me you don't miss them. Chuck and I will be outside in the car. You've got five minutes to get it together and come with us or you can rot here forever." He pointed a finger at me and lifted an arrogant eyebrow. "You've never been a stupid man; I would suggest you don't pick now to behave like one."

With that final declaration, he swept out of the room, taking the electrical current and ominous sense of foreboding with him. I could breathe normally once the space was clear of Nassir's potent charisma and menace. I'd never liked being under the thumb of men more powerful than me, never liked owing them, but if I wanted out, if I wanted a way to make things work, I was going to have no choice but to sell my soul to a devil in a designer suit.

It didn't even take five minutes for me to get dressed, throw the bare essentials into a bag, and hit the front door at practically a run. There was an idling Escalade parked in front of my cabin and Chuck was grinning from ear to ear, his gold incisor flashing at me as I threw myself into the backseat.

He pulled the car away from the cabin and watched me in the rearview mirror. "Fly fishing. I'm telling you boys, we need to find a hobby that gets us out of the city and away from it all. It would be good for us."

Nassir looked over his shoulder at me and smirked. "I have a feeling Benny's had enough of the wilderness. Where are you going to go? New York? Chicago? Vegas? The offer is open internationally as well. You can disappear into wine and women in Paris if that's what you want."

I returned the smirk and turned to look out the tinted window. "The wilderness isn't so bad when you have the right person to hide away with. It's funny that Bax is in Denver because that's exactly where I'm headed when all of this is said and done. There's something there I need to get back." Something like my heart, my sanity, my purpose for being. I also wanted my watch back, now that I was going to have the opportunity to wear it again.

"He's not going to like you being that close to the teenager. You might want to pick somewhere else to hang your hat for the long haul." That warning came from Chuck, but I was more worried about getting to Echo than I was about running into Bax in the Mile High.

"I plan on keeping my head down and my nose clean." I was now among the ranks of those dangerous men who had something invaluable they couldn't afford to lose.

Nassir sneered at me and turned so that he was facing forward. "I'll believe it when I see it, but then again, I never thought you would embrace your inner lumber jack either. I guess anything is possible."

Anything was possible, including the villain stumbling across Snow White and stealing a kiss instead of Prince Charming. Once he woke her up, he simply had to be willing to sacrifice everything he'd ever known and work twice as hard at deserving her.

Chapter 11

Many long, lonely weeks later…

The little boy sitting across from me was the spitting image of his father. He had the same thick, dark hair that had a tendency toward curling, and the same clear, jade green eyes. He even had a single dimple in his cheek, a mirror to his father's, even though his dad's was covered up by a very attractive beard. Every time I looked at Hyde, I searched for some part of his mother, any piece of her she might have left behind in him, but he was all Zeb. Considering the way his mother had been taken from this world, it was probably a good thing the little boy was a miniature version of his old man. Right down to his thoughtful, serious personality that aged him eons beyond his actual years.

"She takes all my toys and she follows me around everywhere." He rolled his expressive eyes as he picked at the pizza that was in front of him. "My dad says I have to be nice to her and share my toys because she's younger than me and I need to set a good example." He sounded as put out as any six-year-old could.

I reached over and snagged a pepperoni off his slice and popped it in my mouth while he fake glared at me. He really was the cutest kid on the planet. "Being nice and sharing are both good things. I think you should probably listen to your old man, Hyde."

He screwed up his adorable face in an expression of youthful indignation. "She's just so loud and messy."

The *she* he was referring to was Remy Archer, the three-year-old daughter of a friend of Zeb's that was indeed a handful, but in the best way possible. Hyde was also her most favorite person in the entire world, next to her parents and little brother. She followed him around like a puppy, begging for attention and throwing a fit when he didn't give her what she wanted. The blonde toddler never met an adventure or experience she wasn't willing to dive head first into and even at her tender age, she was headstrong and defiant. I could see why her wild and rebellious personality was hard to mesh with for a child that was as serious and overly cautious as Hyde was. Remy lived for trouble; Hyde made himself sick worrying about all the ways in which he could disappoint the adults in his life. Losing his mom so young, and in such a preventable and tragic way, had left its mark on the boy, and no matter how fiercely he was loved, those scars would remain.

I reached across the table and ruffled his hair. "Loud and messy can be a lot of fun, Hyde. In fact, most kids your age live for loud and messy. You should embrace the chaos while it's still acceptable." I didn't want him to miss out on any part of his childhood now that he had a stable home life and parents that weren't going anywhere. His mom had stolen too many of his years from him and because I felt the same way about mine and the constant pressure to live as Xanthe's keeper instead of as my own person, I knew he deserved more.

He polished off his slice and gave me a toothy grin when he was done that melted my heart. "I guess she's not so bad, once you get used to her."

"That's the spirit, kid." I glanced at my cell phone and was surprised to see how much time had slipped by. Everything felt like it was going in slow motion since I'd landed back in Denver. Days dragged on, weeks inched by, and hours felt like years as I waited for Ben to come and find me. Time felt like it stood still until I picked up Hyde for our weekly dinner dates. I owed Zeb and his girlfriend Sayer everything for letting me stay in the boy's life when they didn't have any reason to. They didn't have to share the precious time they had with him with a stranger who had made as many bad choices along the way as the woman that abandoned him, but they knew I loved him. They believed me when I said that all I ever wanted was what was best for Hyde, so one night a week, I got to lose myself in the unconditional love of a little boy that made my hurting heart feel whole again. "We should probably pack it in and get you back home. Your dad said you have a project you need to finish for school."

He nodded solemnly and waited patiently while I paid the bill. "I have to write an 'About Me' book."

Winter was fading fast into spring, but it was still chilly enough that I made him put his hat on over his ears as we walked to my brand spanking new SUV. Getting the insurance to pay out on the other one had been a nightmare and that was from someone in the industry. I got Hyde into his seat and strapped in before absently asking, "What's an 'About Me' book?"

He gave a shrug and kicked his feet, which hung way up off the floor. His dad drove a cool vintage truck that earned all the badass points, so my SUV, as fancy and shiny new as it was, didn't impress him very much.

"It's a book that's filled with things about me. Stuff I like, stuff I don't like. I'm supposed to tell the teacher about my family and friends." He made a face that had me laughing when I caught sight of it in the rearview mirror. "I guess I'll have to tell her about Remy since she's technically my friend."

I snorted out a laugh and made my way through the city toward Capitol Hill where all the old, restored Victorians were. "Yeah, buddy, she is your friend, so you should definitely include her. Be sure to mention that you share your toys with her. Never hurts to butter the teacher up."

His eyes locked on mine in the mirror and he tilted his head to the side. "Do you think I should mention my mom? I know she's not here anymore, but she's still up here." He pointed to the side of his head where his little beanie was sitting slightly askew.

I sucked in a breath and willed the spasm in my heart to pass. "If she's in your head and in your heart, Hyde, then she is a part of you. She's always going to have a spot in your memories, both good and bad, but you don't have to share that with anyone else if you don't want to. That can be something that's just between you and her, little man." I hoped that was the right thing to say. I didn't want his son telling Zeb that I was encouraging him to keep something from him, but I knew how closely I guarded the memories I had of Xanthe and now the ones I hoarded from my time with Ben. It was something special that was just mine, something precious that I didn't want anyone else to taint or tarnish. Those memories were what kept me going when the days felt endless and keeping it together felt impossible. I didn't want anyone else's fingerprints all over them, so I wouldn't blame Hyde for wanting to keep the few good moments his mother had given him all to himself.

Hyde stuck out his lower lip and pulled his eyebrows low over his emerald eyes. "I think my mom can stay up here and I'll tell the teacher about Sayer instead. She looks like a princess and makes me pancakes in the morning."

Sayer Cole was the attorney who had enabled Zeb to get custody of Hyde, and somewhere along the way, the buttoned-up, prim and proper lawyer had fallen for both of the Fuller boys. She was everything secure and safe that Hyde needed in his life and I couldn't find an ounce of resentment toward the woman who would be raising my best friend's son. In fact, every single time I was in the other woman's presence, I was inspired to get my shit together and keep it that way. We all owed her a lot, and because she was nothing but class and heart, she refused to acknowledge it.

"I think that sounds like a good plan, little man. Your dad will be all over you telling the world how great Sayer is." I pulled the SUV up in front of the impressive house Zeb had fully restored for Sayer when they first met. It took a couple minutes to get him out of the car and up to the front door, and by the time I had him wrangled, hand clasped firmly in mine, the front door was open and Zeb was leaning against the jamb. The dark hair, flannel shirt, worn jeans, and meticulously groomed beard all reminded me of another man and another place. It almost hurt to look at him. I missed Ben every second of every day. I tried not to let longing and yearning overtake my entire life, but it was a constant struggle. I woke up lonely and went to bed aching. I'd never been a patient person and the more time that passed, the less confidence I had that he would figure out a way to come for me.

Loud and messy was a lot less fun when it came from an adult woman who was holding her life and herself together with nothing more than a hope and a prayer.

Hyde threw himself into his father's legs while prattling on about how he guessed it was okay that Remy made it into his book and how he wanted to make sure he included the fact that our pizza dinner dates were really important to him. Zeb squeezed his son's shoulder and sent him into the house with a smile and a knowing look as I put a hand over my heart.

"He's good at hitting that soft spot without even trying." The big man lifted his eyebrows at me. "You all right? You look a little like you swallowed something sour."

I shook my head and huddled deeper into my jacket. "Still trying to find my footing after losing my sister, ya know?"

That jade gaze missed very little. "Is that so? Because you've been more off since you got back than you were before you left. Normally, I'm not the type to pry, but you matter to my kid. He loves you, and he's had enough people that he cares about let him down, so I just want to make sure you aren't about to go off the rails on us, Echo." He cocked his head to the side and watched me carefully. "You aren't alone anymore."

Good God, did those Fuller boys know how to get right into the center of a heart and turn it all around. I reached up and pushed some of my hair off of my face and managed a weak smile. "I'm not going off the rails or over the edge. Some days it takes everything I have to hold on, but I do it, Zeb. I hold on for dear life. I lost my friend. I lost my sister. I lost my way and my heart." I shifted my feet and told him honestly. "Somewhere in all of that loss, I found myself. I'm not going to let that little boy down and no matter what, I'm not going to let myself down anymore."

I got a terse nod, followed by a hug that swallowed me up. He was such a good man, but instead of envying Sayer for all that she had, his embrace made me long for what I didn't have. I didn't want a hug from a good man. I wanted a bad man to hold onto me and promise that he would never let me go. I wanted him to remind me that his bad made my bad look like child's play and that our good was even more special than most because it had to fight its way to the surface. It did battle to survive inside the wasteland of our tattered souls.

"I'll text you and make plans for next week. I would love to see what makes it in the 'About Me' book when he's done with it. That kid has more going on inside than I ever did. He makes me feel like I still have a whole lot to learn about life and love." I wanted to know what made him happy and see what his new life was like through his eyes. He deserved so much more than he'd been given at the beginning and I wanted to make sure all the adults that loved him were coming through for him, myself included.

Zeb snorted and turned back to the open doorway. "Join the club. I had no idea what I was capable of or how much of myself I could give to another person until he came along. It was like I was sleepwalking and the minute you showed up and told me I was a father, I woke up. I wouldn't have it any other way because I don't want to miss a minute of his life from here on out. We'll see you next week, Echo."

I turned on my heel and made my way back to the SUV with a lump in my throat. I was always emotional after I dropped Hyde off, but I'd been even more so since my return home. Zeb had told me I wasn't alone, but the truth was I very much *was* alone while I waited. No one else knew about the man I'd met on the mountain. No one knew my heart was a million miles away and struggling to beat through pain and desperation. No one knew that I felt untethered and adrift, that nothing seemed worthwhile while I waited to see if I mattered as much to him as he mattered to me. I'd given him an impossible task, one that I logically knew he would need time to accomplish, but the longer he took, the more time that passed, the more I had to wonder if he'd decided I wasn't worth the effort. No one could bide their time or wait for me, so I did it alone and it ate at me. Every day another piece was bitten off and spit out as minutes spiraled into hours that we didn't get to have together.

Just like Zeb, I didn't want to miss a minute of the life Ben had been given a second shot at living, but I was missing millions of them and there was nothing I could do about it.

If I hadn't been lost in my melancholy, I probably would have noticed the very out of place sports car that was parked in front of my apartment building. It was completely impractical for Colorado weather and I didn't live in the best neighborhood, so it was like a beacon calling for every criminal within a ten-mile radius. If I'd taken note of the car, I would have also noticed the faint hint of coconut and honey that lingered in the hallway as I trudged toward my door. My keys rattled in the lock and my breath left my lungs in a whoosh as the door swung open before I could turn the knob. Hard hands gripped my upper arms and I was pulled into my apartment with enough force that my purse went flying in one direction and my keys in the other.

I opened my mouth to scream but never got a single sound out.

Warm lips latched onto mine as those hands curled around my back and pulled me to a familiar chest that was covered in an obviously expensive button-down shirt and bisected by a super soft silk tie. I knew that heartbeat as well as I knew my own. It was the one I dreamed of at night and the one I listened for every moment that I was awake. His facial hair was much shorter than it had been the last time I saw him, neatly trimmed against his jaw and around his mouth. It was all executive and zero lumberjack, but it still felt amazing as it brushed across my chin and rubbed against my cheeks. I'd missed everything about him but the shallow part of me put his beard at the top of the list.

His hair was shorter and more severely styled than it had been in the woods and he'd traded his work wear for a suit that looked like it cost a year's worth of rent. The heavy black boots were also gone and polished wingtips winked up at me from the dingy carpet of my apartment. The gaudy ring on his finger was now joined by another one on his opposite hand and the watch I'd been sleeping with, keeping it stashed under my pillow, was now wrapped around his wrist, looking like it had always belonged there. Everything on the outside was new and unknown, but those gleaming gray eyes and the smirk that told me he knew I was taking inventory and liking everything I saw were all the same.

So was the way he kissed me.

It was ruthless. It was desperate. It was hungry and hard. It was desperate, like we would never have enough time together.

His hands fisted in my hair as he continued to devour my mouth while he walked me backward toward the front door, which he had closed at some point. Once I hit the barrier, he pressed the entire length of his body along mine and finally released my lips so we could both drag in some much-needed air. He shoved one of his legs between mine and untangled one hand from my hair so he could wrap his fingers around my jaw. He brushed his thumb over my lower lip and smiled at me as I lifted both my arms up to wind around his neck. It was the first time I could hold him the way I wanted to and I thought my entire being was going to come apart at the seams from the way I was vibrating with relief and delight.

Now that my head was no longer spinning from fear and excitement, I noticed that he looked thinner and that he had lines fanning out from the corners of his eyes that hadn't been there before. He also had a cut on his cheek that was being held closed with a couple of steri strips and what looked like a healing black eye that had hit the yellowish green phase of bruising. The suit looked good on him. It was obviously made to fit his bulk and build but it did little to hide the stiffness in his movements as he bent forward to touch his lips to mine, softer and sweeter this time.

"Missed the way you taste, Pop-Tart." His fingers dug into my jaw as his breath danced over my now wet and swollen lips. "Missed this smart mouth and all of this hair." He dragged the tip of his nose along the curve of my cheek and touched his lips to my ear. "Missed this soft skin and those long fucking legs." His leg shifted between mine so that my center was pressed tightly against his thigh. "Missed that sweet pussy and those perfect tits of yours, Snow White." He pulled back so that we were eye to eye, both of us breathing hard as we tried to catch up with our racing hearts. "I really just missed everything about you, Echo."

I nodded and tightened my hold on his neck. "I missed you too, Ben." That was an understatement if there ever was one. I felt like I'd been frozen in place and he was the only thing that could warm me up and get me going again.

He grinned at me and shook his dark head. "Not a Ben anymore, babe."

I frowned up at him and he pressed even more fully into me. "What does that mean?"

"It means that Ben can't be here but Nicholas Benton can." He lifted his eyebrows at me. "I think you can call me Benny from here on out and no one would question it because of the last name."

I blinked at him and let out a shuddering sigh. "How did you end up here...Benny? How did you find me?" Denver wasn't exactly a small town and I hadn't given him my address or anything.

He let his head fall until his forehead touched mine. I could feel the weight of the world pressing down on his back but luckily, I was there to keep him upright, to keep him from getting crushed by it.

"Does the *how* matter? It's the *why* that you should focus on." He kissed me again, pushing off the door and taking me with him. "I'm here because you're here, Echo, and that's the only place I ever want to be. Even if it means I have to make deals with the devil."

I gave him a hard look, knowing there was a story there that I was going to need sooner rather than later. He had to know I would take him however he came, and that included tainted and tarnished. Logically it made no sense. We barely knew each other, but somehow, some way we knew enough to know this was it.

"Is there room under your new leaf for deals with the devil?" I gave a yelp of surprise as his hands went to my waist. He lifted me up onto the counter that separated my kitchen from the small living area, and stepped between my legs. His hands skimmed over my shoulders, taking my coat with them as they found their way to my collarbone.

"As it turns out, my new leaf is still attached to the same ole tree. The only thing I care about is that you're under that leaf when it gets turned over." He put his hand over my heart and closed his eyes as it danced against his palm. "Are you going to be there? Can you handle the fact that all I have to offer is fruit from a poisoned tree?"

I waited a beat, a second that had my entire future caught inside of it. If I told him I couldn't handle it, that who he really was wasn't good enough for me, he would go, and I would never see him again. When he got tired of waiting for my answer and pried his long, dark lashes up, I saw the truth clearly in his eyes. He would walk away because he wasn't going to apologize for who he was, but I could also see that he was going to try his best to be a man that no one needed to apologize for.

"I'm right here, Benny. I'm not going anywhere, even if the tree gets chopped down and takes all the leaves with it. I've been waiting for you to find me." And once he had, he'd managed to lead me to myself.

His hand tightened on my shoulder and his eyes briefly closed. He let out a sigh of relief that almost blew me back and when he opened his eyes, I could see that I had given him something he would cherish forever. "I found you in the middle of a blizzard, on the side of a mountain, Pop-Tart. I will always find you, anywhere, everywhere you happen to be." It almost sounded like a threat, but his roughly spoken words made me happier than I'd ever been in my life. I always felt like the people I loved were letting me go and here he was, promising to hold on forever.

He cleared his throat and pulled me closer so that I had to wrap my legs around his waist to avoid toppling off the counter and onto the floor.

"Well, then, we only have one problem left to solve." His deep voice rasped against my skin as his lips touched the pounding pulse point on the side of my neck.

I squirmed against him in anticipation and offered up a breathy, "What's that?"

"How do I get you out of your clothes and get inside of you before I lose my mind? Like I said, I really fucking missed you, Echo. You've been burned into my brain and branded on my heart. The thought of you makes me hard but the reality of having you, of knowing I get to keep you, well, that makes me feel like I'm going to break in half. If there is something more than hard, that's what my dick is right now."

I groaned in anticipation and smiled up at him. "Good thing you've never met a problem you couldn't solve. I'm sure you'll figure it out in no time."

Neither one of us would ever be the kind of people that could be described as good (I was obviously a lot closer to redemption than he was but only because he showed me the way to get there) but there was no arguing that we were great together.

Neither one of us had ever been better.

Chapter 12

Benny

I leaned into her, pushing her back onto the counter, feeling like I was finally right where I was meant to be. She was the promise of everything that could be. She was the fairy tale come to life. She was the dream I got to have while I was wide awake. She was what kept me going, what kept my head on straight when I submerged myself back in the sludge and slime that infiltrated every corner of my hometown. She was the thing that kept me focused when all the familiar temptations that had led me to being a man with no morals and no ethics reared their ugly little heads and beckoned me closer.

She was the reason I had gone to see my mom and tried to make amends and rebuild bridges I'd burned. I tried to tell her I was a changed man, that I was moving forward, making better choices, but too much water had passed under that broken bridge, too many years of her being disappointed in me. She sent me on my way with a goodbye and a "I don't ever want to see you again." She still refused to touch the money that I left in an account for her and, even though the petty part of me was tempted to clear it out and blow it on something extravagant, I refrained. I did, however, clear out all the accounts I had open under an alias the feds had never found and bought myself a new wardrobe, which was a lot like my old wardrobe, and a new car. I was supposed to blend in, but I'd always had a preference for things that stood out. Like Nassir said, I was never a stupid man so I'd been smart with all my ill-gotten gains over the years. I had plenty to sustain my new, legal and legit lifestyle, even if came with the flash and fancy of my old one.

It took longer than I thought it would to get a lead on the girl Nassir wanted me to find. I knew every alley and hole the rats in the Point hid in. I wasn't as familiar with the fancy hotel bars and corporate meeting rooms the guys running the affluent part of the city conducted business in. It was easy to see why Nassir sent me in for him once I got through the glass doors. These guys were all aging, doughy, pale skinned billionaires that would never let a guy with a questionable heritage and known criminal background sully their pristine country club grounds. They really did put the *white* in white collar crime. On the streets, it didn't matter what you looked like or where you came from. The man with the most respect and the baddest reputation was the one in charge, and I had to say I preferred it that way. In the Point, loyalty was earned; here on the Hill it was purchased. Once I was back in my old skin, I fit right in and it only took a few pointed questions, a little bit of blackmail, and one fight with the mayor's paid protection. I held my own but I'd been out of the brawling business for a while, so he got in a lucky shot. By the time it was all said and done, I had a solid lead on the girl and enough information to get the devil off my back—as well as a black eye and some busted ribs.

All of it was worth it, because as soon as the girl was in Nassir's hands, I was free. Well, as free as someone that was going to be spending the rest of their life in WITSEC and at Nassir's beck and call could be. But I was free to introduce the me I was going to be from here on out to my girl and I couldn't wait. I hoped she liked a guy in a snazzy suit, a guy that decided it was time to use his problem-solving skills for good instead of evil going forward.

I slid my hand up the back of her leg and pressed myself into her soft center. Her eyes widened at the feel of my thick flesh against her and her mouth dropped open in a little gasp. I rubbed my nose along the line of her jaw and worked my hands underneath the slouchy sweater she was wearing. Her curls were cut shorter than they had been up at the cabin and I could feel the points of her hip bones and the edge of her ribs as I uncovered her skin. Her bra was a pale pink, made of lace and silk. It was pretty, but not as pretty as the full mounds and pointed tips it was covering up. I dragged my tongue along the lacy edge and curled my fingers around her waist.

"I dreamed about you every night." I slid a hand up her spine until my fingers touched the clasp on her bra. "I jerked off to memories of you in the shower every morning." I popped the clasp open and sighed when I ended up with a handful of warm skin. The velvety point of her nipple stabbed eagerly into my palm and her eyes got heavy lidded and languid. "During the day, I would wonder what you were doing. I couldn't stop worrying about you. Were you finally grieving for your sister? Did your shoulder heal right? Were you taking care of yourself? Were you waiting for me?" I bent my head and kissed the upper swell of each of her breasts, biting down on one so that my teeth left marks on her perfectly pale skin. I wanted to devour her. "I was consumed by you, obsessed. It made me feel crazy. I would've done anything to get back to you." I licked up the line of her throat and stopped to nibble where her pulse was pounding under her skin. "When I was younger, all I wanted was power and respect. I wanted everyone to know I was someone, that I had made something of myself."

I pulled back and trailed my fingers over her breastbone and straight down the center of her body until I reached her belly button. I dipped a finger inside, which made her giggle until I curled it under the waistband of her jeans. "I want you more than any of that, Echo. I don't care if a single soul on this planet knows who I am or the things I'm capable of doing, as long as you know. All I want is you, Pop-Tart."

She lifted her hips so I could get the denim down around her backside. I had to step back so I could pull the jeans down her long legs. My dick immediately missed the soft cradle it had been in and my blood went thick and hot at the sight of all her creamy skin. She really was the only thing I'd ever gotten exactly right in my life.

"Well, I want you too, Benny…but I'm going to be honest and tell you that I want more than that." She blinked up at me as she reached for my tie so she could pull me back toward her. The silk tightened around my throat and made me swallow hard.

I put my hands on the counter next to her naked hips and leaned down so that my forehead touched hers. "If I can give it to you, I will."

"Oh…you can give it to me, all right." She snickered at me and wiggled her eyebrows up and down comically, which made me laugh, something I hadn't done much of before her. "But first, I want you to promise me that if we're in this, we are in it for real. No hiding all the ugly bits and pieces, no pretending things are working if they're not. I've lost so much of myself trying to hide from things that hurt me, Benny. I don't want to hide anymore. I want to be wide awake for every second of this. The good, the bad, and the ugly…I want all of it and I want to know you want all of it as well."

I nudged her legs farther apart and slipped my thumb between her wet folds. She was slippery and all kinds of liquid heat against my fingertips.

"Well, you've got me, so the bad is covered." I swirled my fingers around her stiff little clit and then pushed them into her warm channel. Her entire body spasmed around the invasion and all her muscles tightened. "I have you, so the good is more than covered." I bent so I could kiss her, sweet and slow, which was the opposite of the way I was stroking my fingers in and out of her body. She shifted on the counter in front of me, hips lifting as her hand fisted my tie in a death grip. "Neither one of us has anything very nice to look at in our pasts, so I think we have the ugly nailed down as well. We have it all covered, Echo, and whatever else comes our way, we'll handle that as well."

She blinked up at me and I saw her sigh slow and steady as she moved on my hand. "Good, because between the two of us, I think we can handle anything."

I grunted in agreement. "Is it all right with you if I get on with handling you, Pop-Tart?" She was the only thing I wanted to take care of from here on out. She was the solution to every problem I'd ever personally faced.

She let out a laugh that sent sparks off in my heart and nodded her head before tossing it back as I started to nibble on her neck. "Have at it, Nicholas."

I growled against her skin and sank my teeth in as a warning. "He's the guy that I am when I walk out the door because I have to be. In here, with you, I'm Benny because I get to be."

She scraped the fingers of her free hand along the short hair at my temples and held my biting mouth to her. "Okay, Benny, do your worst."

I chuckled and scissored my fingers around her clit. "No, Pop-Tart, you get my best...always."

I pulled the stiff, pink peak of her breast between my teeth and flicked my tongue over the pebbled skin. It made her shudder and had her legs lifting to wrap around my waist as she undulated against me. She was ready to ignite, her fuse lit from thousands of miles away just waiting for me to show up so she could blow. She was better than any dream I'd had, better than the memories that wound me up and set me off. The sounds she made, the way the blue in her eyes burned, the way she melted against me, the way she pulled me closer and pulled me in, I couldn't get enough of it. It made it obvious I wasn't ever going to spend a moment without her again.

She released my tie so she could get her hands on the buckle of my belt. God, it was nice that she had full use of both her hands. It meant I didn't have to let go of the hold I had on her to help her as she worked the zipper down and pulled my cock out. We both let out a sigh at the contact and I felt her pulse on the inside as her slickness coated my fingers. My dick twitched at her touch and I felt my balls tighten as pleasure settled at the base of my spine.

It felt like it had been months since I'd had my hands on her. It felt like I needed to relearn every dip and curve of her body—and she was clearly relearning every line and ridge of mine as her fingers rolled over every single inch of my throbbing cock. It kicked in her hand, the tip getting just as wet and ready as the place between her legs where my fingers were still steadily fucking in and out of her. I used my thumb to circle her clit, to press down on it and tap as she worked herself into a frenzy, her hold on my erection tightening and sliding up and down in a desperate rhythm. My hips moved involuntarily into her as my heart tried to battle its way out of my chest. It would sacrifice itself for her no questions asked; I would sacrifice myself for her.

I pulled my fingers out of her, dragging them across her thigh and leaving a wet trail as I did. I took a minute to dig a condom out of my wallet and handed it to her with the gruff order to get me covered. She barely had the latex rolled down to the base, her fingers tightening when I pushed into her welcoming heat. Her walls fluttered around my width and her warmth sank into all the places inside of me that were always cold and empty.

She moaned as I swore. She pulled me closer, the silk tightening around my throat like a noose. She panted against my lips as I smashed them against hers, twisting my tongue around and swallowing down my name as she chanted it over and over again. I didn't need to breathe because she was breathing for me. She exhaled all her pleasure and passion into me and it filled me up so much that the fact she was choking the life out of me with her hold on my tie barely registered.

My hips bucked into hers, my hands holding her still on the counter as I pounded every lonely minute, every absent second away. I rode her hard and unforgiving. There wasn't any room for anything other than the blinding need I had to be with her, to be a part of her. I was going to leave fingerprints on her hip and bite marks on her breasts. I was going to leave my heart in her hands and what was left of my soul wrapped around hers.

I dropped my forehead to the center of her chest and chased a droplet of sweat that rolled by with my tongue. I curled my arm where her back was arched and wrapped my fist around where she was still holding onto my cock. I squeezed it tighter, telling her I was close, trying to hold off the inevitable finish so this moment would last as long as it possibly could.

She rocked up into me, her head falling backward, her thighs holding my waist in a death grip. She locked around me like she was never going to let me go and then she let out a long wail and went molten all around me. The force of her pleasure ripped my own from the hold I had on it. We broke together, shattering all over one another, and when we picked the pieces up, there was no telling which ones belonged to me and which ones were hers. They were the pieces that made us. I needed hers and she needed mine in order to be complete.

"I don't know if my heart is any fonder because of our time apart. I mean, it was already as fond as it could be, but it sure as fuck made my dick harder." I pushed up off of her and lowered my face to hers so I could kiss her smiling mouth.

"I like you in the suit, Benny. You look good but maybe next time you can take it off, though I do like the tie. You can leave that on." She used her hold on it to pull herself into a sitting position and then she slid down the front of my body so she could tug me in the direction of her bedroom. I'd found it when I picked the lock earlier and went looking for my watch. I couldn't believe she'd left it under her pillow where anyone could walk off with it.

If I had been her, in her shoes, I would have hocked the damn thing and moved to a better neighborhood. She was moving; she just didn't know it yet.

"Well, I got a new job so I have to dress the part." I let her lead me like a puppy toward the bedroom, watching the sway of her ass and the dimples at the base of her spine like I hadn't just been buried inside of her as deep as I could go.

She looked over her shoulder at me and lifted an eyebrow. "You got a new job?"

I nodded and reached out to wind one of her curls around my finger. "Yeah. Turns out I'm really good at getting into the places where the bad guys who pretend to be good guys do business. Those guys need problems solved even more than the guys who don't bother to hide how bad they are."

She scowled at me but I held up my hands in surrender before she could lay into me about going back to my old ways. "I've got a new handler with the Marshals. He seems like a decent enough guy and he found you for me when I asked. I told him I would be happy to be an informant for him if he needed me to be. I'm not good at many things but I am good at knowing who has the power and the lengths they will go to keep it. I can get in places they can't and I already have a sleazy, shitty history that those entitled money men will never question."

Her eyes got big but she didn't protest when I tumbled her to the bed. She started tugging on my tie and working on the buttons on my shirt. "You're going after the wolves in sheep's clothing."

I nodded. "I am, but those wolves are more like house pets. They don't stand a chance against a guy like me. I figure it won't hurt to earn some karmic brownie points now that I have a reason to behave. I had a good run working for the bad guys; might as well see if I can make a difference working for the right side."

"It sounds dangerous, even for the Big Bad Wolf." She pushed my shirt off my shoulders and let out a gasp when she saw the kaleidoscope of bruises on my side where my ribs were still healing.

"Being under Novak's thumb was dangerous. Getting locked up

was dangerous. Making a deal with the devil was dangerous. Being stranded with no reason to live in the woods was dangerous. Selling out rich CEOs and crooked government officials is going to be a walk in the park. Besides, I have you to come home to and I promise I will do my best to never let you down." I cupped her face in my hands and gave her a kiss that had every promise I intended to keep within it. "You've lost enough, Echo."

She nodded solemnly, and I noticed a sheen of moisture in her pretty eyes. "Good thing you're hard to kill, Benny."

"I had a purpose for sticking around, Pop-Tart. I just didn't know that reason was you until you came crashing into my life." I kissed her and told her with one hundred percent honesty, "That was the best night of my life."

She made a choking sound and pulled me down by my neck so she could bury her face in the side of my throat. "It was the worst night of my life, but you are the best thing that's ever happened to me."

That night she'd had vengeance in her heart and wanted to avenge her sister so that she didn't have to deal with her grief and pain. I tried to show her that the best way to honor the memory of those she's loved and lost was to live the best life she could. She deserved forgiveness for her past sins and she deserved acceptance and happiness moving forward. She deserved a man who would fight for her, and fight against her when she tried to run.

I was going to give her the best life I could.

Everything I used to take for myself, I was going to give to her.

I was going to make my second chance count because I knew deep down into my bones that this was the one and only shot I was ever going to get at loving and being loved.

Good thing I got it right on the first try.

The End..........

Discover the Liliana Hart MacKenzie Family Collection

Go to www.1001DarkNights.com for more information.

Discover the World of 1001 Dark Nights

Collection One

Collection Two

Collection Three

Collection Four

Bundles

Discovery Authors

Blue Box Specials

Rising Storm

Liliana Hart's MacKenzie Family

About Jay Crownover

Jay Crownover is the International and multiple New York Times and USA Today bestselling author of the Marked Men Series, The Saints of Denver Series and The Point and Breaking Point Series. She is a tattooed, crazy haired Colorado native who lives at the base of the Rockies with her three awesome dogs. This is where she can frequently be found enjoying a cold beer and Taco Tuesdays. Jay is a self-declared music snob and outspoken book lover who is always looking for her next adventure, between the pages and on the road.

Salvaged

Saints of Denver
By Jay Crownover
Coming June 21, 2017
Go to https://www.jaycrownover.com/ for more information

The *New York Times* and *USA Today* bestselling author of the Marked Men books continues her delightfully sexy Saints of Denver series.

Hudson Wheeler is a nice guy. Everyone knows it, including his fiancée who left him with a canceled wedding and a baby on the way. He's tired of finishing last and is ready to start living in the moment with nights soaked in whiskey, fast cars, and even faster girls. He's set to start living on the edge, but when he meets Poppy Cruz, her sad eyes in the most gorgeous face he's ever seen hook him in right away. Wheeler can see Poppy's pain and all he wants to do is take care of her and make her smile, whatever it takes.

Poppy can't remember a time when she didn't see strangers as the enemy. After a lifetime of being hurt from the men who swore to protect her, Poppy's determined to keep herself safe by keeping everyone else at arm's length. Wheeler's sexy grin and rough hands from hours restoring classic cars shouldn't captivate her, but every time she's with him, she can't help being pulled closer to him. Though she's terrified to trust again, Poppy soon realizes it might hurt even more to shut Wheeler out—and the intense feelings pulsing through her are making it near impossible to resist him.

The only thing Poppy is sure of is that her heart is in need of some serious repair, and the more time she spends with Wheeler, the more she's convinced he's the only man with the tools to fix it.

* * * *

Read on for a sneak peek at the poignant and powerful conclusion to the Saints of Denver series.

Prologue

I was the kind of guy that thought I had it all figured out. It came from having spent my entire childhood caught up in chaos and upheaval. When I was old enough to call my own shots and make my own way, I did it with a single-minded determination and unwavering dedication. I knew what I wanted. Every move I made, every step I took, moved me toward that perfectly planned future I had been dreaming of from the minute I realized I was all on my own. A realization that came far too early and was brutally reinforced every single time I was forced to bounce from one temporary home to the next.

I clung to the idea that I would do everything differently. I would make decisions which would lead to a life that was easy, smooth, and as steady as a car with a new alignment and high-end shocks. I found the girl that was meant to be mine and clutched her in a death grip. I went out of my way to be whoever she needed me to be, to never give her any kind of reason to go. I made her the center of my entire world, not realizing she might feel trapped there as time went on. I was holding on so tight I never felt her trying to wiggle her way free.

I started a business, bought a house, and made plans ... so many plans. Plans that would be considered simple and boring to some, but they covered everything I wanted since the time I was four years old. They were the plans that would give me the life I'd been longing for since I the minute I was left on mine own.

I had my eyes on the prize, the promise of what could be if I worked hard, took care of my woman, and did everything that the person who was supposed to love me and care for me didn't do. I would have held on until the bitter, burning end, but there was nothing I could do when the rope was cut.

At that point all I could do was fall.

I felt my grip on everything I was trying so hard to hold onto slip the day she walked into my garage, hiding behind one of my friends. Rowdy St. James worked at the tattoo shop where I got the majority of my ink done. He called and asked me to empty out my shop of employees and other customers one Saturday afternoon so that he could bring his girlfriend's sister in to look at a car. He didn't need to explain why the garage needed to be cleared out, not that I would have asked. The girl had been all over the news months before. You couldn't get away from her terrified face and shaking body as her horrifying ordeal was splashed all over the media. Her husband had abducted her at gunpoint. Salem, her sister and Rowdy's lady, had been a victim of the attack as well. Poppy Cruz only went with the lunatic to keep her sibling safe, but it had resulted in a nightmare that I couldn't imagine anyone coming back from. Without question cleared out the shop so she wouldn't have to worry about being surrounded by a bunch of dirty, boisterous men that wouldn't know how to behave around someone as fragile and delicate as she appeared to be.

I didn't want her to be scared of anything ever again.

Things at home had been rocky, rougher than class-five rapids in winter, but I was paddling for my life and prepared to ride it out. I couldn't let go. I wouldn't let go. I saw Poppy the day she walked through my shop and I started to feel how sore my hands and my heart were from holding on.

Her head was down, focused on the tips of her shoes. Her shoulders were hunched over and her long hair hid her face. She was skinny, so skinny, nothing but skin and bones. She was nothing that I should have noticed, not because she was clearly doing everything in her power to be invisible, but because I was supposed to have my eyes locked on my future and doing whatever I could to salvage it. But I did notice her and I couldn't look away once I did.

She was obviously terrified, clearly out of her element and uncomfortable, but it wasn't her unease that called to me … it was her loneliness. I could feel it filling up the space that separated us. Stretching, growing, expanding until it was all I was breathing in and exhaling back out. It was bitter on my tongue and heavy across my skin because I knew the feeling well. I lived with it pressing me down and pushing me forward every minute of every day. The reason I was so set on the way things had to be, the reason I was singlemindedly set on settling down and building a life with the girl that was slipping through my fingers was because I never again wanted to be as alone as this girl was. I didn't want to be left and forgotten. I'd barely survived it the first time.

I did my best to sell her a car that was as beautiful as she was … a classic with clean lines and a flawless finish. She picked something practical and boring but that was ultimately safe and reliable. I understood her choice but it grated and annoyed me long after she left the shop. When she wasn't standing in front of me, she should have been easy to forget; after all, everything in front of me, everything I had been working for and toward, was falling down in front of my eyes. My world was collapsing in on itself and everything I thought I was so goddamn sure about turned out to be nothing more than lies and illusions. In the middle of all of it, I couldn't forget her sad eyes and shivering, shaking form. Her loneliness clung to me, unshakable and unforgettable. I didn't think I would see her again and against my better judgment I often found myself wondering how she was doing and if she had gotten a handle on all the things that seemed to be crushing her under their inescapable weight.

I was wrong about seeing her again, just like I was wrong about thinking that doing everything in my life differently from how my mother had lived hers would ensure my happiness and a future built on an unshakable foundation. I was wrong about hard work and sacrifice being enough. I was wrong about holding on when what I was holding on to desperately wanted me to let go. All I was left with was bleeding palms, rope burns around my heart and scars on my soul.

The next time I saw Poppy Cruz it was *my* loneliness that was filling up the space, suffocating me, choking me, making me forget to handle her with care. I was nothing more than a vast, open wound. One that was raw, aching, throbbing, and leaking my heart and shattered emotions out everywhere. I felt like I'd lost everything, like my entire life had been nothing but a waste of time, nothing more than building blocks knocked over with the swipe of a careless hand. The girl I loved didn't love me back, my future was ultimately nothing more than a fuzzy, fractured blur. I couldn't see anything clearly other than waste and ruin.

But I saw her. And I saw that I scared her.

It was the last thing I wanted to do but my loneliness was just as big and just and consuming as hers was. It spread out, hungry and angry, looking to consume anyone that might try and challenge its reign.

I tried to pull myself together, apologized because I knew our paths would cross again now that she lived next door to my best friend. I didn't want to be another man that she was terrified of. I locked the loneliness down, wrestled it into submission, and tried to quiet down the wild inside of me that was howling, screaming at the loss of its mate. I wanted to be nothing more than gnashing teeth and tearing claws but I swallowed those instincts and allowed myself to be like a kicked puppy that just wanted to whimper and cry.

Poppy that had been through more than I could imagine. She was the one I couldn't look away from, but even then, she managed to slip past me and disappear. She looked like honey but she moved like a ghost. I memorized everything about her even though she hardly let me see her face.

I wasn't supposed to be looking at anything other than how to salvage the mess my life was in, but she was all I could see.

Chapter 1

Poppy

I couldn't believe I was doing this.

I was pretty sure sometime over the last week my body and brain had been taken over by an alien life force that was making me act the opposite of how I normally acted.

Even before I was scared of my own shadow, I wasn't the type that went out of my way to seek attention from the opposite sex. Making boys drool and collecting broken hearts was more up my older sister's alley. I tended to be the girl that only spoke when spoken to. I was always shy and hesitant, especially when I was around someone that I found attractive. I'd had more than one man tell me that it was endearing … little did I know that my obvious uncertainty about my own appeal and allure clearly marked me as prey to those same men. I was an easy target. Something I swore to myself I would never be again. Which was why there was no logical explanation for why I found myself currently parked in front of a very industrial-looking building as I tried to work up the courage to go inside.

The garage was on the outskirts of downtown Denver. Tucked away among factories and buildings that were now gentrified and redeveloped upscale apartments and trendy eateries near Coors Field.

The garage looked like it had escaped every dime of big money sunk into making LoDo prime real estate. It was a throwback to when this part of the city was still rough and unsafe for people to be out walking their little dogs on designer leashes after dark. The bricks on the outside had faded paint from when the garage was some kind of shipping warehouse. The old paint blended in with newer graffiti that the owner hadn't bothered to power-wash away. There was also a mural, a beautiful depiction of the Rocky Mountains, that stood off in the distance; it covered all three of the massive metal doors that allowed the cars access in and out of the building. It was a statement piece. One that was impossible to miss. It softened the entire feel of the building and the tall metal fence with its wide gate that surrounded it.

I knew that one of the guys who owned the tattoo shop where both my sister and her boyfriend worked had painted the mural in trade. Wheeler, the guy I was here to see, if I ever got up the nerve, worked on Nash Donovan's muscle car and in turn Nash had turned the garage doors into something that even the most dedicated taggers and graffiti artists appreciated too much to deface. Salem, my sister, mentioned that Wheeler was never opposed to a solid trade. Which explained why the majority of the mechanic's skin was painted and inked in colorful images courtesy of Nash and the Saints of Denver tattoo shop.

I was used to being surrounded by heavily tattooed individuals—heck, my sister started marking her permanently tan and golden skin before she was legally old enough to get a tattoo in order to annoy my father. However, Hudson Wheeler was by far the most decorated human I had ever come across. The designs swirled up each side of his neck and across his throat. They dropped down over his wrists and splayed wide across the back of his hands. He had artwork across his chest and it crawled from the base of his hairline all the way to the top of his jeans across his back. He was a walking art installation., And while all that ink and color might have been overwhelming on someone else, with the graceful, thoughtful way he moved and the quiet, measured way he spoke, all the color and noise that covered his body worked for the man that was known as Wheeler. . I figured out after the first time I met him that his skin was telling the world his story because he didn't want to be bothered with repeating it over and over again.

My father would be appalled by the way Hudson Wheeler looked. He would hate everything about him. Clearly that meant I allowed the trickle of attraction that had worked its way through the fear and doubt that suffocated me on a daily basis to take root and grow. Anything that my dad disapproved of was something that I was more than willing to embrace with open arms.

Taking a deep breath and tapping my fingers on the steering wheel, I looked over at the little box that was on the seat next to me. A small grin tugged at my mouth when my eyes landed on the contents. I had no idea if Wheeler was in the market for this particular kind of gift but I figured if he didn't want it I would take it home until I figured something else out. It was a bold move, bringing a man I hardly knew this kind of gift, but as soon as I saw it I knew Wheeler had to have it.

I scolded myself for being foolish and impulsive, silently telling myself that I was setting myself up for the kind of embarrassment and ridicule that would cripple me. It had taken me close to a year in therapy and unwavering amounts of tough love from my family and friends to get to the point where I could leave the house without having a full-on panic attack. Taking a step so far out of my comfort zone felt like I was jumping off a cliff without knowing if there was anything down below to cushion my fall. If Wheeler rejected the gift, if he made me feel stupid for trying to do something nice, it very well might undo all the hard work I'd put into getting back some semblance of a normal life. Trying to cheer up a man that I had no ties to or no investment in seemed like a foolish risk to take, but I still packed up the box and drove down here. I tried to talk myself out of going inside, my mind screaming that this was a mistake. It didn't work. Even though I was a nervous wreck I still ended up grabbing the box, making faces and muttering under my breath at the contents like they could reassure me this wasn't going to blow up in my face. I was shaking from head to toe as I exited the car.

The box shifted in my hold, which made me gasp and mutter a few choice words. My father would hate that I was swearing, so I made it a point to do so at least once a day. I had to shut the car door with my hip and I jumped when it slammed shut. I watched wide-eyed as one of the painted metal doors started to roll up. I squinted behind the dark lenses of my sunglasses as a lone figure walked to the edge of a bay and deftly jumped down, ignoring the ramp that led up into the building. I gulped a little bit because there was no mistaking the tall, lean figure that was making his way toward me. The late-afternoon sun made his already burnished hair glow like autumn fire, and highlighted the dips and valleys in his arms and across his broad chest as he wiped his hands on a red rag that he pulled from his back pocket. He had the top half of his coveralls unfastened and hanging around his waist, leaving him and all that artwork that covered him on display in nothing more than a black tank top that had a hole on the side. He looked dirty and a little rough. Both things totally worked for him … and for me. I'd almost forgotten what lust felt like. I was attracted to him and that terrified me because in my world attraction led to nothing but heartache and hurt. Still, here I was, standing in front of him even though everything inside of me was screaming to run as far away from him as possible.

I moved as the box shifted again and stopped as he lifted his chin up in the direction where I had parked my very nondescript sedan. "Something wrong with the Camry?" Wheeler's voice was warm and smooth, like expensive liquor sipped on summer nights, but his eyes were cold. They were the palest blue I had ever seen, a blue so washed out and light that they had a silvery shimmer to them. They were also sharp and intent, not missing much, including the box I was having a hard time keeping a hold on as he got closer.

"Um … no. The Camry is fine, thank you." Rowdy, my sister's boyfriend and the father of my soon-to-make-an-appearance niece or nephew, had strong-armed me into buying a car from Wheeler when I finally decided I was emotionally well enough to live on my own after I fell apart at the hands of the last man that was supposed to love me. Wheeler tried to sell me a 1957 Bonneville that was hands down the coolest car I had ever seen, but I balked at the idea of riding around in something that was guaranteed to attract unwanted attention. Especially attention of the male variety. Rowdy cringed when I handed over the cash for the Camry but Wheeler just smiled like he understood why I made the choice even if he didn't think it was the right one.

I nervously shifted my feet and watched as that icy gaze of his landed on the box clutched to my side. Right on time the contents let out a little half bark, half yelp that had Wheeler's eyebrows lifting up almost to his hairline and made his tattooed hands pause where they were still wringing the red rag tightly between them.

"Is that a puppy?" He sounded curious and slightly amused, which I took as a good sign. Most of the men I'd dealt with in the past would have been furious that I had not only showed up unannounced but did so with a tiny, wiggling puppy in tow.

"It is a puppy ... I ... uh ... well, someone dropped them off at the vet's office where I work and I thought that since Dixie is leaving and taking Dolly with her, and you seemed so fond of her that maybe you wanted one of your own ... well ..." I was rambling and talking too fast but I couldn't stop the words from rushing out one after the other. Dolly was my neighbor's pit bull, my neighbor who just happened to be Wheeler's best friend. "Plus, you own a house, so you can have a pit bull or maybe you need him as a guard dog for the garage. With some training, he could be perfect. You can take him to work with you, which is great since most puppies have to live in a crate while they're being trained." I shifted my feet again and looked down at the dog, who was whining up at me like he felt sorry for me because even a nonhuman could tell I was making a mess of this. "Pit bulls are illegal in the city limits so we have to adopt them out because shelters will euthanize them if we can't find them homes, and no animal deserves that."

He didn't answer me but he did reach out and take the box from me. The brindle-and-white puppy immediately jumped to the edge of the box and started yipping at and sniffing the new person that was within licking distance. Wheeler put the box on the ground and picked up the solid little body and held the adorable animal up in front of his face while the puppy barked excitedly and wagged his stubby little tail. "He's cute."

Oh lordy, was he ever ... and I wasn't talking about the dog.

"Um ... I know it's kind of presumptuous but I thought maybe you two could help each other out." I cringed as I unwittingly stumbled into personal territory where I absolutely didn't belong. It had been nothing more than bad timing and admitted curiosity that landed me right in the middle of Wheeler's personal life imploding. I shouldn't know that his now-former fiancée had cheated on him, prompting him to cancel the wedding only a few weeks before they were set to walk down the aisle, and I also shouldn't know that this wasn't the first time his woman had stepped out on him. But I did know and it had me feeling all kinds of ways about what he had been through. I knew that Wheeler was a nice guy, one that deserved a bit of happiness while he healed from that kind of devastating heartbreak. And really, who couldn't be happy when they were holding a puppy, especially when that puppy was already clearly in love with him.

"I'm going to miss Dixie more than I'm going to miss Dolly." He gave me a crooked grin as he mentioned my neighbor.

The fact that I lived next door to Dixie was the reason I knew all the gory details of his recent breakup. She was his ex-fiancée's sister as well as his best friend. The walls were thin and Dixie was one stranger that I trusted enough to get close to, so I spent a lot of time at her place. It sucked that she was getting ready to move to Mississippi right when Wheeler needed her the most. But her boyfriend was there and she missed him, so it was obvious she wasn't happy being in Denver when Church wasn't.

I cleared my throat and lifted fingers that had a visible tremor in them to my hair. I pushed some of it behind my ears and winced when the motion knocked my sunglasses sideways. I didn't know if I could handle this conversation eye to eye but it was move the sunglasses or look like more of a spaz than I already did. With a sigh I pushed them to the top of my head and froze as his frosty eyes locked on mine. They were so cold I should be frozen from the inside out . . . instead I suddenly felt warm all over and heated in way that was foreign and strange. I'd never been so physically drawn to anyone before and it made me both anxious and agitated. I didn't know what to do with it. I wasn't in any kind of place emotionally to be crushing on a guy with the kind of complicated history and tangled future Wheeler had. I was only recently able to take care of myself in the most basic of ways There was no way I had it in me to take care of him as well ... and that's what he needed ... a woman that would step up to the plate and fix all the things that selfish and thoughtless woman had broken. A woman who was selfish and thoughtless. A woman he very well might still be in love with.

"If you don't want him I'm going to ask Dixie to take him. Dolly can always use a friend. One of my coworkers took home his sister and the doc I work for found homes out of state for the other two boys in the liter. This little guy was the last one that needed a home. I couldn't stand seeing him left alone while the rest of his family found forever homes. Like I said . . ." I shrugged a little and looked away from that piercing stare. "I immediately thought of you." Wheeler was looking for his forever home too I just knew it.

He bent down and put the puppy on the ground. The stout little animal started to jump on his lower legs and nipped at the worn leather of his sturdy and stained boots. Wheeler put his hands on his hips as he watched the puppy. I was almost a hundred percent certain that bringing the abandoned ball of slobber and love had been the right call when those arctic-colored eyes lifted back up to me. His expression was hard to read but it was clear something was stopping him from embracing my gift with open arms.

"I don't know that I have the time to take on a puppy right now, Poppy." He lifted a hand and rubbed it across the back of his neck. His mahogany-colored eyebrows pulled into a vee over the top of his nose and the corners of his mouth pulled down in a frown that was too harsh for his pretty face. I liked it much better when he smiled and his twin dimples cut deeply into his cheeks.

I bit my bottom lip to keep the distressed noise that I could feel climbing up the back of my throat at bay. I knew he might say no but I couldn't hide the fact that I was disappointed by his decision. I honestly felt like he and the puppy would be good for one another, that they could bring a little joy into each other's life. It broke my heart a little that Wheeler wasn't ready to open his heart up again, even when it was to something that was so obviously eager to love him unconditionally and irrevocably, unlike his ex.

"It's okay, Wheeler. Like I said, I'll take him home until I can find a place for him. I'm sure Dolly could use a friend." I crouched down and wiggled my fingers to get the dog's attention, and grinned when he bounded over, tripping over his front legs as he scrambled in my direction. "I can take him to work with me and hold on to him until I figure something out. One of the boys at the shop will step up if Dixie doesn't want another dog."

I heard him sigh and looked up to see him watching me intently. He opened his mouth like he was going to say something, then let it snap shut with his teeth audibly clicking together. I didn't know much about Wheeler, but what I did know I liked. He was nice. He was polite. He was thoughtful and he was kind. But more than any of those things, he went out of his way to hold himself in a way that wasn't threatening or intimidating because he was aware without me saying a word how jumpy I was around people, men in particular. I hated that they were bigger than me. I hated that I knew firsthand how badly they could hurt me if they had a mind to. I hated that I wilted and cowered under their attention, even if it was innocent and friendly. The fact that he took care not to spook me spoke volumes and made me feel awful for putting him in such an awkward position.

"Poppy …" He sounded regretful and I had no interest in dragging the torture out any longer for either of us. I scooped up the dog and buried my nose in the top of his head.

"Seriously it's no big deal. I love him and I'm happy to wait until I can find him a proper home. It was stupid of me not to consider how busy you are with everything you have going on in your life right now. A puppy is a big commitment and that's not something you can put on someone else without discussing it with them first." The dog swiped his tongue across my face, no doubt feeling my distress and rising panic. I wanted to tuck his warm little body to my chest and run away like I was trying to score a touchdown in the other team's end zone. "I should have known better." That was a common refrain, one that chased me into nightmares and blasted through my head every single second I struggled to survive at the torturous hands of my abusive husband. I found myself repeating dangerous, harmful patterns where the men in my life were concerned, and through it all I told myself over and over again that I should have known better. My therapist would tell me I was being too hard on myself, that I was shouldering the blame for the actions of men that I had no control over.

Wheeler made a noise that sounded like he was choking and then bent over at the waist so that his hands were resting on his knees as his breath wheezed in and out. His wide shoulders shuddered and then tensed like he had taken a blow that knocked the wind out of him.

I didn't touch anyone, not even the people that had grown up hugging me and loving me. But I was compelled to reach out a shaky hand and put it on his colorful shoulder. The puppy gave a yip of approval and I tried not to fall to my knees as the warmth from his tattooed skin blazed through my fingers and shot up my arm. It had been a long time since I'd let myself have any kind of human contact, and even longer since that kind of contact didn't leave bruises and welts on my skin and tattered lesions across every surface of my soul. He felt so vital. So necessary.

"Are you okay?" The shoulder I was lightly touching tensed even tighter and I let go like his skin burned me when he righted himself and I ended up frozen in that frigid stare of his.

"No. I'm about as far from okay as I have ever been." He let out a brittle-sounding laugh and narrowed his eyes at me. "When a pretty girl shows up trying to make the shit show that has become your life better, it should be okay, but it's not."

He sighed and rubbed a hand over his face like he was tired. "I can count on one hand the times in my life someone bothered to ask if I was okay, Poppy." His mouth twisted into a wry grin that would look harsh on anyone else but with those dimples of his still managed to look downright adorable. "Most of those times have been Dixie asking. It wasn't even the right sister."

I was horrified and didn't bother to hide it as I huddled the wiggling puppy to my chest like his warm little body could protect me from the images his awful words brought to mind. "That's terrible, Wheeler." My voice shook and the words sounded squeaky. I already knew too much about him and this was more information that I didn't feel like I had earned the right to have.

"It is pretty terrible but not nearly as bad as my ex telling me that she's knocked up with my kid." I gasped and took a step backward as his words landed like blows. "A kid we definitely didn't plan on. A kid I am in no way ready to raise with a woman I can't stand to be around. A kid that is going to have to bounce between houses and be shuffled from one place to another always trying to figure out exactly where home is."

He sounded shattered and he looked the same. Those eyes of his were colder than anything I'd ever seen, his skin was pale and taut over the sharp angles of his face, making the smattering of freckles that dotted his nose and cheeks stand out even more than they normally did.

A baby.

Those words always hit something delicate and unprotected deep inside of me. When my sister first told me that she was expecting a baby, I wanted to be happy for her but that happiness had to fight its way through remorse and sorrow so thick it felt like it was crushing me. The same thing was happening as Wheeler watched me. Everything inside of me wanted to unravel but I was holding it together, barely. He should be happy that he had a precious little life on the way, even if he was less than thrilled with the circumstances surrounding the arrival.

I took another step backward and almost fell over. Wheeler reached out a hand like he was going to catch me or stop my fall, but I flinched away and tightened my hold on the dog so much so that he yelped in protest. Frantically I pulled my sunglasses from the top of my head and shoved them back over my eyes. I could feel moisture building, and if I started crying I needed something to hide behind. He wouldn't understand why his words stripped me bare and I didn't have it in me to explain the reasons why they cut so deeply. I'd used up all my limited courage and nerve getting myself out of the car and offering up the puppy.

"Well, congratulations on the baby." I didn't sound like I meant it even though I honestly did. "I'm gonna take this little guy and head home and make some calls about who might be in the market for a puppy."

I scrambled back some more and watched wide-eyed behind my sunglasses as Wheeler advanced on me. He followed me until my back was flat against the side of the car and he was looming in front of me with only the puppy to separate his chest from mine. It was the closest I had been to a man in a very long time, and even though he was irritated and riled up, I couldn't say that I was worried about him taking out his feelings on me.

"I'm sorry, Poppy. If I was in a different place in my life I would be pretty fucking excited that a girl like you had me on her mind and went out of her way to do something really sweet for me. If I wasn't already struggling to get my head around being a new father, I would happily take on the task of being a puppy parent." God, he was nice. Even when he was looming over me looking not very nice at all. "There's something about you, something about those eyes and the soft way that you speak, that makes me want to tell you all my secrets. Secrets that sting, like the fact that the last time my life was this fucked up was when my junkie mother was dropping me off at a fire station in some rinky-dink mountain town in the middle of a snowstorm. Our car broke down, because it always did. She didn't take care of it and she sure as shit didn't take care of me." I felt my mouth drop open in shock but couldn't move as his voice dipped lower and his eyes got even colder. His words sent shivers up and down my spine.

"I was lucky that it was a manned station and not one of the volunteer houses that sits empty until a fire is called in. There was a very nice fire captain there that took me in for the night. The next day I was dumped with child services and I spent my entire childhood jumping from one foster house to another. She didn't even have a coat for me. She dropped me off in jeans that were too small, a T-shirt that was stained and torn, and in tennis shoes that were shit for the snow because they were mostly duct-taped together." He blinked at me as I gasped in horror and that harsh scowl that cut into the pretty lines of his aristocratic bone structure was back. "I was fucking four years old."

I wanted to hug him. I wanted to comfort the little boy he was and the man that was clearly struggling in front of me. Knowing that I would freak out if we actually made that kind of contact while both of us were so raw, I scooted to the side, careful not to brush up against him, and pulled open the door so I could put my panting, slobbering bundle down in the passenger seat. I kept the door between us as a barrier as I nodded vigorously. All I wanted to do was get away from his desperation and pain. I needed to take a minute to process the fact he had a baby on the way with a woman that had destroyed him and ruined the idyllic life they could have had together. That hurt in ways I didn't want to pick apart while he was standing so close looking at me like he could see right into the center of my every thought and feeling. I had too much of my own hurt; I couldn't believe that I was feeling his as well.

"I'm so sorry you had to suffer like that. Good luck with

everything, Wheeler." I couldn't bring myself to tell him I would be around if he needed me, even though the words were tickling the tip of my tongue. I slipped into the car and wrapped my fingers around the steering wheel like it was some kind of lifeline. I reached for the door to pull it shut but it wouldn't budge because his hand was wrapped around the top of the frame. He bent his head to look down at me and I could see a riot of emotions blowing through his cool gaze. He was pissed. He was frustrated. He was sad. He was irritated and he was maybe, just maybe, a little bit excited.

"Gonna need more than luck. But seriously, thank you for thinking of me. I don't think I can remember the last time someone did that." If I was someone else, someone stronger, braver, someone fearless instead of fearful, I would have climbed out of the car and given him that goddamn hug. He looked like he desperately needed one.

But I wasn't someone different.

I was the girl that had almost died trying to make her father happy and win his approval.

I was the girl that let her sister leave without begging her to take me with her when that was all I really wanted.

I was the girl that fell in love with the wrong boy and paid a price so heavy for it that I lost everything.

I was the girl that married a monster, and even though the demon was physically dead and buried, he still lived inside of me, where he haunted me, hounded me, hurt me.

As always, I was afraid, so I didn't do anything other than shut the car door when he let go and drive away. I really couldn't fix all the things that were wrong with Wheeler's life and I wasn't about to let him close enough to see exactly how broken my own existence was because I'd yet to be able to fix myself.

The puppy whimpered like he knew what I was thinking and disagreed with me. Luckily, he was a lot easier to ignore than the taunting voice in the back of my head that kept up the steady refrain of *You should have known better.*

On behalf of 1001 Dark Nights,

Liz Berry and M.J. Rose would like to thank ~

Liliana Hart
Scott Silverii
Steve Berry
Doug Scofield
Kim Guidroz
Jillian Stein
InkSlinger PR
Asha Hossain
Fedora Chen
Kasi Alexander
Pamela Jamison
Chris Graham
Jessica Johns
Dylan Stockton
and Simon Lipskar

Printed in Great Britain
by Amazon

86559410R00082